Delilah Doolittle
AND THE
Missing Macaw

Patricia Guiver

BERKLEY PRIME CRIME, NEW YORK

DELILAH DOOLITTLE AND THE MISSING MACAW

This is a work of fiction. Names, characters, places, and incidents are either the product of the author's imagination or are used fictitiously, and any resemblance to actual persons, living or dead, business establishments, events, or locales is entirely coincidental.

A Berkley Prime Crime Book / published by arrangement with the author

PRINTING HISTORY
Berkley Prime Crime edition / February 2000

The Penguin Putnam Inc. World Wide Web site address is http://www.penguinputnam.com

ISBN: 0-425-17342-9

Berkley Prime Crime Books are published by The Berkley Publishing Group, a division of Penguin Putnam Inc., 375 Hudson Street, New York, New York 10014. The name BERKLEY PRIME CRIME and the BERKLEY PRIME CRIME design are trademarks belonging to Penguin Putnam Inc.

PRINTED IN THE UNITED STATES OF AMERICA

10 9 8 7 6 5 4 3 2 1

For

The Dolly Sisters—a lovebird, a dwarf parrot, and a cockatiel—and Woodstock, the crested canary. They winged their sweet way into my heart and left too soon.

And for
Bogart

and the volunteers of Basset Hound Rescue of Southern California.

Acknowledgments

The inspiration for this tale came from an article in *Animal People,* a watchdog publication ever on the alert for animal exploitation in all its cruel manifestations.

My thanks for sharing her expertise to my friend Cheryl Rendes, of Wonders of Wildlife, who finds her bliss in teaching us to cherish all creatures, no matter how slimy, scaly, or scary looking.

And, as always, my thanks to the staff at the Orange County Animal Shelter, particularly Director Mark McDorman, Kennel Chief Al Garcia, and Lieutenant Mary Van Holt, who continue to answer my questions with unfailing courtesy and good humour.

A robin redbreast in a cage
Puts all Heaven in a rage

—WILLIAM BLAKE

Delilah Doolittle
AND THE
Missing Macaw

• 1 •

The Floater

"WATSON! COME HERE!" But the offshore wind threw the words back in my face, and the big red Doberman romped on along the beach, past driftwood washed ashore by the previous night's storm, past the accumulated plastic picnicware, beer cans, babies' nappies, and other disposable miscellania at which one didn't care to look too closely, entwined with the seaweed gathered at the water's edge, and continued on blissfully unaware of the sign by the pier that warned NO DOGS BEYOND THIS POINT.

My old tennies squelching along the waterline, I hurried to catch up with my dog before we were ticketed for violating the leash law. Not that anyone was about. The lifeguard towers, recently refurbished in readiness for the busy summer season, were not yet manned. Or perhaps one should say "personned"—several women had recently qualified for Surf City's elite lifeguard corps, though as far as I knew, no *Baywatch* babes had yet applied.

It was early morning, and except for an elderly gentleman feeding the seagulls farther down the beach, we had the place to ourselves. The man was wearing earphones and would be quite unable to hear the gulls screeching as they swooped above his head, diving to grab morsels from his gloved hand.

Red flags were posted, warning swimmers of dangerous riptides. An unusually late spring storm, the result of El Niño, had churned the surf to an uninviting roil, and left behind an overcast sky.

Despite a wind that had my hair standing on end and my eyes smarting from salt spray as Pacific waves hurled themselves against the shore, I was enjoying the outing. It would take considerably worse weather than this to keep Watson and me from our morning walk on Dog Beach, sometimes called Tar Beach for the seepage from nearby oil fields onto this least desirable stretch of Surf City's ten-mile strand.

Watson finally came to a halt under the pier and started to sniff at what appeared to be a large piece of driftwood bobbing at the water's edge.

I stopped to catch my breath. It was quieter here. The fury of the waves abated as they broke against the pilings, and their roar, mingled with the cooing of pigeons roosting in the pier's underbelly, created an odd symphony. Heavy spray washed the uppermost reaches of colonies of blue-gray limpets clinging to the pilings. It would soon be high tide.

"What've you got there, Watson?" I was surprised she hadn't looked up at my approach.

I moved in closer, the water lapping over my ankles, and was shocked to see that it was not driftwood that she nosed so curiously. A body floated in and out at the water's edge, facedown, arms stretched toward the beach as if still grasping for a life hold. Sodden clothing, perhaps a sweatsuit of indeterminate colour; bare feet; probably young, for I could see no grey in the long black hair that floated around the head.

I jumped back in horror as the next wave lifted the body farther onto the beach, almost depositing it at my feet. The sweatsuit jacket shifted in the eddying water and I glimpsed what might once have been a young, tanned back. Glimpsed also, in the folds of clothing, what I at first took to be a streak of blood, but which on second glance turned out to be a long, sand-encrusted, red feather.

• 2 •

The Old Bill

I LOOKED AROUND for help. To summon the police was imperative. To stay here in case the poor unfortunate floated out to sea again, equally so. I stepped out from under the pier and waved at the elderly gentleman still feeding the gulls.

"Hallo! Over here!" I shouted. But even if my words had not been lost on the wind, he could not have heard me over those earphones.

Turning seaward, I saw a lone surfer, obviously undaunted by warnings of riptides and heavy currents, negotiating a huge wave, nimbly shifting his feet to adjust to the whims of wind and water. Then, knees bent, one foot in front of the other, arms balancing, he entered the curl, emerging long seconds later to slide effortlessly down the wave, then adroitly lowering himself to sit astride his board. Before he had a chance to turn toward the horizon to watch for the next set, I waved furiously with both arms.

He started to paddle his board shoreward, no doubt none too delighted to have his sport interrupted. As he waded ashore, board under his arm, I saw that the neoprene-clad figure was none other than Tony Tipton, a.k.a. Tiptoe Tony, an erstwhile colleague of my late husband.

" 'Allo, Mrs. D," he greeted in his familiar Cockney accent. "What's up, then?"

"You're taking a chance, aren't you?" I chided. "Didn't you see the red flag?"

"No. Didn't see a thing." Tony's grey eyes twinkled in his tanned, lined face. He was an expert surfer, a senior champion, in fact, and though one might have expected his advancing years to bring caution, even now, in his seventies, he continued to take chances. But Tony was no stranger to risk. I'd heard he'd taken many in his career as a small-time crook—a career from which he now claimed to have retired.

"Waves are the best they've been for weeks. They're breaking way out by the oil rig," he went on as he followed me along the sand. "What did you drag me in for? It'd better be good."

"You may well ask. Come see for yourself." I led him back under the pier to where Watson continued to stand guard over the waterlogged body.

"Cor blimey," said Tony, taking in the tragic scene. "If that ain't a turn-up for the books!" Tony had lived in America for thirty years or more, but he sounded as if he still had the dust of Ellis Island on his shoes. "Poor sod probably got caught in the rip."

He could be right. Only that morning I had read in the *Los Angeles Times* that the strong southern hemisphere storm had shifted the ocean bottom, producing pockets of treacherous rip currents.

"But fully clothed?" I said.

"You're right. Well, maybe he fell off the pier, or got swept off the rocks while he was fishing. Been in the water several days, by the looks of 'im." Tony sat down on the sand and removed his surf booties. "I'd better go and get help."

Leaving his surfboard propped against a piling, he took off for the nearest telephone, up on the pier, leaving me to join Watson in standing guard. I clipped on her leash. A flock of officials would soon be arriving; it wouldn't do to have a loose dog adding to the confusion.

Tony was back quicker than I expected. He hurriedly collected his board, saying, "I'm taking off, luv, before the old Bill gets 'ere." His chequered past made him prone to be the first suspect in any questionable circumstance. Face-to-face encounters with the law were to be avoided whenever possible.

This time he was out of luck. A red Chevy lifeguard truck had arrived, and by the time Tony had informed marine safety officer Tim Hager of what had occurred, the police were already trudging across the beach. In the personages of, I was dismayed to see, Detective Jack Mallory and Sergeant William Offley of the Surf City Police Department's homicide division.

I hadn't seen Mallory since the end of the Careless Coyote Affair. I had been at home recovering from exhaustion after a rather foolhardy but ultimately successful attempt to save a litter of kittens from a burning house, and he'd very kindly brought me flowers. I had refused his invitation to lunch, pleading a sore throat, but had been sincere when I'd suggested "another time." The fact that I hadn't heard from him since suggested that his offer had been made purely from a misplaced sense of duty. Having been rebuffed, he was off the hook.

"Mrs. Doolittle," he said upon recognizing me. "What are you doing here?"

"I found him," I answered somewhat diffidently, indicating the lifeless form at the water's edge. I would very much have preferred to be elsewhere, having been involved in a few too many of Detective Mallory's investigations over the past couple of years. He might have been forgiven for suspecting that I went out of my way to do so. But in every instance it had been pure coincidence that my search for a missing pet had led me to cross paths with Detective Mallory on the trail of a murder suspect.

Sergeant Offley was reporting in over the police radio. "We have a floater. Under the pier. A John Doe."

"Do you know this person?" Mallory asked me.

"Good heavens, no. The first time I set eyes on him was less than an hour ago."

"But you know it's a male?"

"I don't *know* any such thing, but to judge from the clothes, the hair, the physical appearance . . ."

A sudden gust of wind whipped chill around our heads. Impatiently Mallory brushed his grey hair, a little longer than I might have thought acceptable for a police officer, out of his blue-grey eyes. He was dressed in dark grey slacks and navy blazer. I wondered idly if his choice of pale blue shirt and blue-and-grey paisley tie, so complimentary to his colouring, had been deliberate. But I immediately dismissed the notion as uncharitable. Whatever his faults, which included a certain brusqueness and a tendency to think the worst of people, qualities, one supposed, only to be expected of a policeman, Jack Mallory was not a vain man. Rather, I attributed his excellent choice to an inherent good taste. He wore his clothes to advantage, despite being a little on the heavy side.

I was suddenly conscious of my own appearance. Though I have been known to dress well on occasion, and have, in fact, an excellent wardrobe, due to the influence of my friend Evie, style is not what I have in mind when I take my dog for a run on the beach. Old sweats and sports shoes are far more serviceable. As now, with my tennies full of water. I looked at Mallory's black loafers, covered with damp sand. He followed my gaze, and responded with a rueful smile, encouraging me to inquire, "Why are *you* here? I thought you were with the homicide division."

"All unexplained deaths are regarded as homicides until investigation proves otherwise," Mallory explained patiently. "This could turn out to be an accidental drowning, or it might be murder or suicide. The body's already started to decompose, so it may be hard to determine the primary cause of death. We'll have to wait for the coroner's report. Meanwhile, we'll see if missing persons can give us a lead."

While we were talking the paramedics had arrived, along with the deputy coroner, looking strangely out of place on the beach in his business suit. Groups of onlookers began to gather. Above on the pier, passersby leaned over the railing for a bird's-eye view, while below, surfers and early-morning joggers stood a short distance from the crime scene, which had been cordoned off with orange cones and yellow tape carrying the black-lettered caution POLICE LINE. DO NOT CROSS. A warning a few curious surfers managed to circumvent by paddling out into the ocean a few yards, then returning to the beach within the restricted area.

Much to the frustration of Officer Offley. "Clear the beach of all unauthorized personnel," he ordered. But no sooner had one pod of surfers been hustled back into the water than another approached.

Wiping his brow, struggling to walk with authority

through the spongy sand, the burly policeman approached Mallory. "Male, possibly Hispanic, no personal effects or ID," he said.

"What about the feather?" I said, pointing to the red plume still sticking from the pocket of the man's sweatpants.

"What about it?"

"It could be a clue." The words were out before I considered just how irritating Mallory might find my unsolicited advice.

"Mrs. Doolittle, just look at the debris the storm has tossed up along the shoreline," he replied, a little too condescendingly, to my mind. "The feather could have come from anywhere."

Tim Hager, standing nearby, agreed. "The ocean's been throwing up everything. We've got rocks, palm fronds, trash, you name it."

"Including bodies, it seems," I said, not to be put off by either one of them. "Well, the feather certainly came from a red bird, and I know of no red seabirds." I turned to Mallory. "You're a birder. Am I right?"

I could tell from Mallory's expression that I had overstepped the mark. The blue-grey eyes, so cordial a few minutes earlier, turned cool. He closed his notebook, indicating that our interview was at an end.

"We'll need your statement, Mrs. Doolittle," he said. "Can you come down to the station as soon as it's convenient? You know where it is." Was that a dig at what he considered my past interference in police business? I hoped not. I would not have counted sarcasm among his faults.

I was relieved to be dismissed. Pulling on Watson's leash, I was turning to leave when Mallory spoke again.

"Oh. Just one more question. Were there any other witnesses?"

I gestured toward Tony, standing a few feet away talking to a group of surfers. "Tony, er, Mr. Tipton, was here, surfing. I hailed him in to the beach and asked him to go for help."

At the sound of his name, Tony joined us.

"Any idea of the victim's identity?" Mallory asked him.

"No, guv. Probably not from around 'ere. With the strong riptides an' all, he must've fallen in and drifted from up the coast a ways."

"Or it could have happened right here in Surf City," put in Offley, looking up from his notebook.

"But he wouldn't just stay where he fell in. Use your loaf, mate," said Tony.

Baffled, Mallory raised bushy eyebrows at me, requesting translation.

"Use your head," I explained. "Loaf of bread—head. It's Cockney rhyming slang. The phrase is abbreviated."

"I see," said Mallory, who quite obviously didn't see at all.

"Any old 'ow," said Tony, ignoring the interruption, "just because 'e washed up 'ere don't mean this is where 'e fell in or got shoved in."

"Any other witnesses?" asked Mallory.

"Only the man feeding the seagulls," I said.

"What man?"

I turned and pointed down the beach. "Right over there."

But the elderly gent had vanished.

♣ 3 ♣

Tony's Place

"SOMETHING ABOUT THAT bloke looked familiar," said Tony.

We were waiting to cross Pacific Coast Highway, after which we would go our separate ways: I to my cottage a half mile from the beach, Tony to his trailer park, almost immediately across from the pier.

"What bloke?" I asked, pulling Watson's leash in tighter as we hurried at the "walk" signal.

"The one what was drowned."

I was puzzled. "I thought you told Mallory you didn't recognize him."

"Well, I'm not sure, like. And even if I was, I'm not going to let on to 'im, am I? Stay as far out of it as I can."

I let that pass. "Anyway, I don't know how you could tell, considering the condition he was in."

He shrugged and changed the subject. " 'Ow's the pet detective business going these days? Still chasing after them dogs and cats?"

Though he might tease me, Tony, a pet owner himself, was one of the few people of my acquaintance who appreciated, or even understood, what I did for a living.

"And birds," I said. "There's a message on my machine right now—I haven't answered it yet—about a lost parrot of some kind. I'll have to do my homework so I'll know what I'm looking for. If I take the case, that is. Finding dogs and cats is one thing, at least they keep all four feet on the ground. But a lost bird . . ." I shook my head. "Up, up, and away. It could be anywhere by now."

"One of me neighbours, Bobbi's 'er name, she's got all kinds of birds—parrots and the like. She might be able to 'elp you."

Tony stopped abruptly as we reached the curb. "That's it!" he said, snapping his fingers. "That drowned chappie! He reminded me a bit of Joe, a pal of Bobbi's son, Little Bob. I think I'll pop in and ask if they've seen 'im lately. Wanna come?"

I hesitated, not at all sure I wanted to have anything to do with anyone even remotely connected with Detective Mallory's case. But the woman lived nearby; it would be foolish to pass up the opportunity to learn something about the bird fancy.

"She collects exotics?" I said.

"If that's what you call 'em. Budgies, canaries, cockadoodle whatsits."

"Cockatoos?"

"Them, too. Bloody row they all make first thing in the morning. Don't bovver me none. I'm up early and off surfing. But some of the neighbours, them 'oo likes to sleep in, they don't 'arf get narked. Not that any of 'em dares say anything. They're all a bit scared of 'er. Mind you, she is a bit of a caution. You must have seen her riding around town on that there motorbike of hers. Usually got 'er dog in 'er backpack."

I had to admit that was one of the sights of Surf City

that had thus far eluded me. But I was intrigued. This Bobbi person sounded interesting.

We made our way through the run-down trailer park, home to retirees, fishermen, summer renters, and free spirits like Tony. There were still signs of the devastating fires of the previous autumn. Many of the home-owners had not carried fire insurance and had only partially restored their homes. Now, barely recovered from one disaster, the residents had to contend with another of nature's furies—El Niño generated high tides. Many of the homes were barricaded with sandbags to protect against flooding.

"I'll just pop in and say 'allo to me dog first," said Tony as we approached his trailer. "You'd better come, too. Trixie'd be right miffed if she knew you and Watson came by and didn't stop in."

Trixie, Tony's Jack Russell terrier, had heard our approach and was barking excitedly at the door.

The single-wide mobile home had been completely restored after the fire and shone with a new coat of paint. The tiny front yard had been relandscaped. Either Tony was extremely handy, or he had sufficient means to pay a contractor. I wondered again, as I had often done before, about his resources. A monthly Social Security cheque would not support this kind of expense. Nor the vintage Ford woody station wagon—after Trixie, Tony's most cherished possession—parked on the concrete slab alongside the house.

Tony unlatched the gate in the low white picket fence and propped his surfboard against the trailer's metal siding alongside several others of varying sizes, colours, and shapes, from which I understood he would choose depending on surf conditions. Mounting the steps, he unlocked the front door and we entered a small living room to Trixie's boisterous greeting.

"Where's me dog, then? Did you miss your old dad, then?" Tony said as the little white, black, and tan terrier ran circles of joy around him, stopping now and then only long enough to greet Watson and me with a cursory sniff.

"I'll just go and change out of me wet suit," said Tony, disappearing into the next room. "Make yourself comfy. Shan't be a tick."

I looked around the sparsely furnished room. Tony's needs were minimal, but what possessions he had were immaculately tidy. A sparkling picture window offered a magnificent view, interrupted only by the traffic on PCH, of a wide stretch of beach and the storm-tossed Pacific blending into the blue-grey horizon beyond. No need for Tony to check the daily surf report. He had only to look out the window.

Newspapers and surfing magazines were stacked neatly on a low wicker table beside a comfortable re-cliner upholstered in maroon corduroy. On top of the television console at one end of the room stood several trophies attesting to Tony's prowess on the waves.

The kitchen was equally neat. A single teacup and saucer stood on the counter; a tea towel bearing a picture of Regent's Palace and the legend *a present from Brighton* lay over the sink. A saucy, suggestive cartoon post-card from Blackpool was attached to the refrigerator door with a surfboard-shaped magnet.

Trixie's food and water bowls sat on a plastic place mat under the kitchen table. I recalled that Tony had told me he served in the British navy during World War II. I had been raised in the British Isles, a seafaring na-tion—Britannia rules the waves and all that—and had never known a sailor who wasn't almost obsessively tidy.

I thought with embarrassment of my own cluttered house. I was congenitally unable to throw anything away. Stacks of newspapers and magazines containing articles and recipes to be clipped and filed in yet unpurchased organizers awaited my attention. Dispirited houseplants jostled for shelf space in haphazard display, seeming to rebuke me for their neglect. My closets were more likely to contain bedding for the occasional orphaned dog or cat, or temporary housing for the injured wildlife which might show up on my porch, than to reflect any real desire for order.

Had I been too quick to judge Tony because of his unorthodox lifestyle and questionable manner of supporting himself? Tony lived by his own code—"Taking care of number one," to be precise—and I tolerated his acquaintance out of a possibly misplaced loyalty to my dead husband, Roger. They had been colleagues in a dubious enterprise, the details of which I had yet to fully comprehend. Now, seeing Tony's living quarters for the first time, I also saw another side of him.

" 'Ere we are, then," said Tony, emerging from his bedroom in black OP shorts and a white T-shirt proclaiming SPURS RULE, in honour of the Tottenham Hotspurs, his favourite soccer team. The hairs on his spindly legs, bleached from the sun and faded with age, showed white against his tan. His feet, gnarled with surf bumps, clung to faded blue rubber thongs.

"Okay, Trix," he said to the little dog waiting expectantly by the door. "You can come this time. But watch out for that nasty Spike."

"Who, or what, is Spike?" I asked as we made our way over two rows of trailers to the bird woman's house.

"You'll see. Better keep a tight 'old of Watson, too."

♣ 4 ♣

Biker Chick

A SHAR-PEI IN a red wig; that was my first impression of Roberta "Bobbi" Briscoe. A flabby five-foot-five or so, pale blue eyes almost disappearing into a puffy wrinkled face, heavy chin thrust forward beneath a small flat nose, she could have easily passed for sixty, though Tony had told me she claimed to be in her fifties. A black Harley-Davidson tank top displayed to disadvantage the bird tattoos covering the ample flesh of her arms and upper torso. Khaki shorts "fit where they touched" as the saying goes. Too short and too tight, they looked decidedly uncomfortable around the crotch, as I was unfortunate enough to observe since she was up on a ladder when we arrived, painting the outside of her trailer a quite bilious shade of green.

At Tony's friendly "Hi, Bobbi," she put down the paint roller and stepped down the ladder to greet us, the untied laces of her worn combat boots flapping dangerously.

All smiles, she enveloped Tony in a bear hug, as if greeting a long-lost lover.

"You old son of a gun," she said, futilely attempting to wipe paint from her hands with a rag. "Where've you been hiding yourself?" Her gravelly voice told of too much smoke and spirits.

Easing himself out of her grasp, Tony introduced me. "This 'ere's Delilah Doolittle. She's a pet detective. I bin telling 'er about yer birds."

A guarded look of something unfathomable—disdain or scorn, surely not jealousy—flickered across Bobbi's face as she nodded hallo. If she thought of me as a rival for Tony's affections, she had another think coming.

She motioned for us to sit at the redwood picnic table which took up most of the tiny front yard. Tony sat astride the bench seat; I perched on the end. Trixie and Watson sat patiently at our feet.

"Wanna beer?" asked Bobbi, reaching into a red ice chest under the table and handing Tony a can of Coors Lite. "See, I got your favourite."

I knew for a fact that "light" anything was not Tony's choice. His preference was a pint of mild and bitter, only to be had in these parts at the Pig 'n' Whistle, an expat Brit club.

Bobbi turned to me, offering a beer. Silver and turquoise rings looked painfully tight on her fat fingers.

I shook my head. "No, thank you." No alternative being offered, and the social niceties out of the way, I smiled and said, "Tony tells me you're a bird collector."

Bobbi grinned and, with a wink at Tony, said, "Collector? I guess you could call it that."

As if in confirmation, the squawking of what must have been at least half a dozen parrots, soon accompanied by a high-pitched yapping, broke out from inside the trailer. Trixie and Watson were on their feet, barking and alert for trouble. Any further attempt at conversation was ended for the time being.

"You woke up Spike," said Bobbi accusingly, above the din.

She went inside the trailer and returned with a small black dog under her arm. Squashed between its owner's chubby biceps and folding bosom, the toy poodle peered at us through cataract-shrouded eyes. A tiny pink tongue lolled from its mouth indicating that most of its teeth were gone. Despite the dog's unlikely name, I guessed from the magenta polish on its nails that it was a female. She had recently been groomed, and a faint aroma of cologne lingered. Was this the notorious Spike that Trixie and Watson had been warned against?

We soon found out.

Bobbi put the little dog on the ground, where it immediately charged at Watson, yapping with all its tiny might. Watson uttered a low growl, but otherwise took the unprovoked attack good-naturedly enough, thinking, no doubt, that this aged harridan was beneath contempt.

Crouching down, I attempted to make the proper introductions and was rewarded with a nip on the arm. Near toothless Spike may have been, but she nevertheless managed to break the skin. I hoped she'd had her rabies shot. But it was not serious enough to make a fuss. Bobbi obviously thought so, too, since she made no attempt to apologize, or even to offer a plaster.

I was surprised, though, that she didn't scold the dog, saying only, "She's a bit short-tempered. Doesn't like being woke up." She snapped the cap off a can of beer and poured some into a dish. "This'll calm her down."

Spike lapped at the brew eagerly.

"You all right, luv?" asked Tony with concern, holding a wriggling Trixie in his arms. He had picked her up, obviously intent on keeping her out of harm's way, but she was eager to get down and enter the fray. I did my best to protect Watson: holding her on a short leash with one hand while dabbing at my wound with a tissue with the other.

"I'll live," I joked.

"Well, you can't say I didn't warn you. About Spike, I mean."

Bobbi watched this exchange of pleasantries with obvious annoyance and, with the excuse of bringing another beer, came around to Tony's side of the table and put her arm around him possessively.

Accepting with good grace what I was sure was an unwelcome display of affection, Tony took a sip of his beer, wiped his mouth with the back of his hand, and asked, "Little Bob about?"

"He's around here somewhere. Took Mary for a walk." Bobbi looked down the road. "Ah, speak of the devil . . ."

I turned to see a young man approaching. He was in his late twenties, I would guess, wearing a white T-shirt, faded blue jeans, nothing on his feet. On a rope thick enough to tow the *QE2* he dragged an old pit bull, her pendulous teats almost brushing the ground as she walked. Far from living up to her breed's fierce reputation, her spirit seemed quite broken, no doubt a result of having been bred, I was to soon learn, every time she came into season.

If I'd given the matter any thought, I might have expected Little Bob to be a younger, more masculine version of his mum. I would have been wrong. As slender as she was heavy, his belt barely held his jeans up over his narrow hips. His long, untidy blond hair, which he had the annoying habit of shaking off his face in an almost girlish gesture, framed shifty eyes and a weak mouth and jaw. He sported only the one tattoo, and that misspelled, of a curling wave and the words SERF CITY. I wondered if he was aware of the error.

As Little Bob leaned down to take the rope from the dog's collar, the pit cowered as if expecting a blow. He dragged her into the backyard behind a chain-link fence, Spike nipping at her heels as they went. Mary yelped and hurried through the gate, further encouraged by a kick from Little Bob. Fortunately he was unshod, or he would have heard from me.

"About time you took that dog to the pound," Bobbi said when her son rejoined us. "That last litter were a bunch of runts. Cost more at the vet's than they was worth."

Her son mumbled something about having sold the pups for seventy-five dollars apiece at the swap meet, and reached across the table to help himself to a beer.

He ducked, almost falling against the trailer's wet paint, as his mother slapped his arm. "Not now, son," she said. "Clean up after the dogs first."

Little Bob picked up the poop scoop leaning against the fence and followed his dog into the backyard. "All right, all right. Give me a chance. I just got back."

Clearly, the only resemblance Little Bob bore to his mother was in his attitude toward Mary, treating the poor dog in much the same bullying fashion as his mother treated him.

Bobbi shrugged and turned her attention to Tony.

"We've missed you, Tony," she said, simpering. "Thought you'd forgotten all about your best girl."

Sheepishly Tony looked down at the beer in his hand. He is one of those people who never met a stranger, and I guessed that Bobbi had misinterpreted his friendliness as a come-hither signal.

He moved to the other side of the picnic table, ostensibly to have better access to the cooler. But Bobbi sidled after him, almost tripping over her boot laces as she went.

"Can we go have a look-see at the birds?" Tony said, in an obvious attempt to distract her.

"Go on in," said Bobbi, nodding to me. Tony made as if to come along, but Bobbi's chubby hand kept a tight hold on the lean little man's shoulder. "Me and Tony have some catching up to do."

Tony winced, but couldn't release himself without appearing rude.

I handed him Watson's leash, and made my way up the steps into the trailer.

"Be sure to close the door," Bobbi called after me. "Don't want the birds getting out. And don't pay Fred no mind."

5

For the Birds

WHO WAS FRED? An attack parrot, perhaps? After Spike, I thought I was prepared for anything, but there was yet another surprise in store.

The interior of the single-wide trailer was in stark contrast to Tony's bachelor austerity. Cluttered and untidy to the point of slovenliness, it was stuffy and smelled of unwashed dishes, bird droppings, and cheap scent. The biggest difference was in the light—Tony's windows had opened onto the bright prospect of beach and blue horizon; Bobbi's musty curtains were drawn against the midday sun.

My eyes adjusting to the gloom, I observed, at the far end of the narrow room, the elderly gentleman I had seen on the beach earlier that morning. He was dozing in a maple rocker, the earphones around his neck. Worn leather gloves lay in his lap. This must be Fred.

Trying not to awaken him, I checked out the parrots. Housed in small cages, they differed in size and colour but were all alike in evidence of feather plucking and self-mutilation. I was far from being an expert, but I understood such neuroses to be symptomatic of boredom, poor diet, and neglect. There were no labels on the cages to identify what types of parrots they were, but I was reluctant to call on Bobbi to tell me about them. It was a relief to be out of her company for a few minutes. I found her coarseness repellent, and was determined to leave as soon as I decently could.

The birds had started nattering again, disturbing the old man's nap. He woke up looking confused and worried.

"I didn't touch 'em. I didn't, I didn't!" he cried.

"Of course you didn't," I said gently. "It was my fault. I set them off."

"Bobbi gets real mad at me if I touch them, or try to feed them." He looked anxiously over my shoulder as if expecting Bobbi to appear. "She says I leave the cages open, and they get out. Maybe I do. I can't remember. But they need attention, and I ain't got nothing else to do all day."

Obviously he loves birds, I thought. That's why he feeds the seagulls. There's no one at the beach to object.

"Joe lets me take 'em out," he continued. "But he ain't been around lately."

Joe. That must be the young man Tony thought he recognized as the drowning victim.

"I saw you at the beach this morning," I said.

"Oh, yes. Been going down there every day for almost forty years, excepting for service in World War Two."

"You must know the area well, then," I said.

"Knew Surf City when it was called Oil Town. Them were the days. Oil boom changed everything." His voice weakened and he appeared lost in thoughts of days gone by. "Now it's all people and houses, houses, houses . . ." His eyes closed and I thought he was dozing off again, but as I turned to leave, he started to speak.

"The seagulls, they look for me. And they show me stuff."

"Oh. What kind of stuff?"

"Things people leave behind. Found a watch one time, and money. And today I found . . ." He reached into his pocket as if about to show me something, but changed his mind.

"Mustn't let Bobbi see," he mumbled. "She'll take it."

Before I had a chance to encourage him to show me his treasure, he drifted back to his nap.

I sighed. This visit had been a waste of time. There was nothing here for me. I should have known better than to take Tony's word for anything. A well-stocked pet store would have yielded more information.

I felt I'd seen all I cared to of lonely old men and dispirited parrots, and tiptoed out so as not to set any of them off again.

I returned to the front yard to find Tony, Bobbi, and Little Bob sitting around the picnic table playing cards. Under the table Spike lay on her back, her little painted claws extending upward, her head to one side, pink tongue lolling out. She was snoring—sleeping off the beer, no doubt.

Watson and Trixie, obviously bored, snapped at flies, stopping occasionally to have a good scratch. I suspected fleas. I intended to give Watson a good bath as soon as we got home. I was prepared to leave as soon as I could make a graceful exit.

But just then, as if he'd been waiting for my return, Tony started to tell Bobbi and her son about the body on the beach.

"Thought it looked a bit like Joe, that mate of your'n," he said, dealing the cards. " 'As 'e bin around lately?"

Little Bob looked at his mother as if seeking permission to say something.

"Couldn't have been Joe," she said. "He hasn't been here for a couple of months. He said he was going to visit his folks out of state somewhere."

Seemingly emboldened, Little Bob added, "Last time I saw him was—" He stopped as Bobbi shot him a withering glance.

"I thought I told you to put the trash out," she said.

I decided Tony must have been mistaken. Both Bobbi and her son seemed convinced that it couldn't have been Joe whose body washed up on the beach, and in that case, their indifference was not really surprising. Suicides, and accidental drownings—usually inlanders unused to the vagaries of the ocean's rips and currents—were, unfortunately, not uncommon.

Bobbi threw down her cards, ready to change the subject. "You met Fred, our boarder?" she asked me. "His family pays me to keep an eye on him while they're at work. Sleeps most of the time. Good thing, too. Alzheimer's," she said, tapping her forehead, as if suggesting mental retardation. She really was offensive.

"He seems very fond of the birds," I said.

She shrugged. "Can't let him get too attached. I don't keep 'em long." She went on to explain that she took birds from people who no longer wanted them and found them new homes. Here at last was something I could relate to. It was an all-too-familiar pattern. I regularly heard from people who, having obtained a pet in a moment of impulse, soon found it to be too much trouble to care for and started looking for someone to take it off their hands.

Bobbi added that she also bred birds for trading at local swap meets. "I've got them in back. Wanna see?"

She led the way to the far side of the house past an old grey Dodge van to a small aviary, where finches, cockatiels, and parakeets were crowded together with no regard to species. The portable cage, about five feet high, its base set on wheels, was made of wood and chicken wire, its hinged sides and top allowing for easy folding and transportation.

Alongside the aviary stood the Harley-Davidson motorbike Tony had mentioned. It might well have turned out to be a classic had one been able to see beneath the grease and grime. As it was, it appeared barely roadworthy. A bug-encrusted windshield, cracked in several places, seemed as if it would be more of a hindrance than help. Attached to the bike was a rickety sidecar, its dark green paint badly chipped, the little door, tied shut with string, barely keeping its contents, a haphazard assortment of birdcages, from spilling out. More cages were stacked in an orange-crate trailer on kiddy trike wheels which was attached to the sidecar by means of a short length of chain. Altogether, Bobbi's favoured mode of transportation was a very dodgy-looking contraption indeed.

At the rear of the yard stood another, larger aviary, the front of which was covered with a tarpaulin. "You have more birds over there?" I asked, making a move in that direction.

"No. That's empty," Bobbi said hurriedly. She turned toward the front yard. "I think I heard Tony calling you. Better get back."

I hadn't heard a thing, other than the twittering of the small birds. However, I was as anxious as she appeared to be to end the tour, and I happily followed her.

"My dad had a motorbike and sidecar something like that," I told Tony as he walked me back to the trailer park entrance. "Though he kept his in tip-top condition. It was his pride and joy. I used to ride pillion when we went to the scrambles at Brand's Hatch." I referred to the hillclimbs in England.

Tony's eyes grew round in disbelief. "Cor. That's something I'd like to 'ave seen. Our Mrs. D on an 'Arley."

He continued to rib me and I regretted having confided in him. There are some things, like first love and other youthful indiscretions, to which a woman in her middle years would be well advised not to call attention.

♣ 6 ♣

It's So SoCal

WITH A WAVE to Tony I walked the short distance along PCH, Watson eagerly leading the way, and turned right on to my street just north of the pier. Like many of my neighbours, I had taken advantage of the city's offer of free sandbags as a precaution against El Niño's flooding rains and exceptionally high tides, and the rain-soaked white bags, some split open by the force of the previous night's storm, lay untidily against the base of the house.

My feeling of unease, however, had nothing to do with any havoc El Niño might have caused. It was more immediate. My grisly discovery at the beach that morning weighed heavily on my mind.

Who was that young man, and why had he come to such a sad and untimely end? If it was suicide, what would lead one so young to such desperation? Worse was the suspicion that he might have met with foul play. I thought about his family anxiously awaiting his return, and wondered if they had filed a missing-persons report.

I shook my shoulders as if trying to shake off my malaise. Detective Mallory would get to the bottom of it, I was sure, and I was determined to try to put it out of my mind. I had responsibilities of my own to take care of.

It was past noon. Out on the back porch Hobo, the three-legged ginger-tom feral who condescended to allow me to feed him on occasion, was sunning himself on the chaise longue, contemplating the birdbath where half a dozen sparrows splashed, sending sun diamonds of water over the surrounding paving stones. Sensing Hobo had murder on his mind, I sent Watson out to create a distraction. The birds dispersed in tweets of alarm, and Hobo, not one to bear a grudge, jumped down to greet his friend, rubbing his lean, sleek body along the big red dog's flank. There was no making a pet out of Hobo, who considered all of the wetlands his personal domain, but he and Watson had developed a cordial relationship which belied the traditional enmity of cat and dog. Their friendship could be traced to the time when Watson had alerted me to Hobo's plight the day he'd been caught in a steel-jaw trap. The cat had lost a leg but gained a friend and a refuge as a result of that agonizing experience.

Leaving them to enjoy the spring sunshine, I sat at the kitchen table with my lunch of Marmite sandwich and cup of tea, and caught up with news in the *Los Angeles Times*. I was in need of diversion and soon found it in a calendar listing of lectures and seminars. On offer this week I could choose from the ABCs of Aromatherapy, How to Make California sushi roll, and Aliens or Us. All very New World, not to mention New Age. An art class on folding money into the shapes of, among other things, frogs and rosebuds, sounded only slightly more promising. Unfortunately, I couldn't hang on to my money long enough for that particular talent to serve any useful purpose. The only use I had for folding money was for paying bills.

I emptied the teapot, saving the damp tea leaves to

mulch my favourite yellow rosebush outside the front door, and turned to the post. Mostly bumf—adverts and circulars of no merit whatsoever other than to make me wonder yet again why it was necessary to sacrifice so many trees in the name of commerce.

An insurance-company solicitation offered coverage against flood and earthquake. Surf City was located not only on a major floodplain—it seldom rains in Southern California, but when it does it is often of biblical proportions—but also on the major Inglewood-Newport earthquake fault line. To be insured against these calamities was not exactly a waste of money; in fact, not to do so was probably quite foolhardy. But there was no use worrying about something I couldn't afford. My job as a pet detective barely provided enough to live on, and but for the occasional monetary gift from Great-aunt Nell in darkest Sussex, I probably wouldn't be able to afford to hang on to my little forties beach cottage, my husband's only legacy.

My education at an exclusive English girls' school had endowed me with every art and grace save that of earning a living. After Roger's death, I had been at my wit's end as to how to support myself, when a stroke of luck had led me to finding a lost dog in Las Vegas. Word of mouth had led to other requests for my services, and I eventually set up shop as a pet detective—an occupation requiring limited investment and wardrobe, no skills, in fact no qualifications whatsoever, other than a love of animals, a natural curiosity, and a tendency toward eccentricity. Furthermore, I can work at home, and take my dog with me whenever I have to make business (that is, shelter) trips. In fact, I discovered that a career as a pet detective has much to recommend it in ways of job satisfaction, though little in terms of income.

I put aside the Sierra Club and Audubon Society newsletters to read later. To paraphrase Thomas Jefferson, the price of open space is eternal vigilance, and I kept my eye on the wily ways of developers and transportation agencies, always ready, at the drop of a tax dollar, to throw another freeway across our diminishing wilderness areas.

Of more immediate concern were the lost-and-found flyers I received regularly from the animal shelters with whom I networked throughout California and the Southwest. One in particular caught my attention as being within my bailiwick.

REWARD:
Lost while on Vacation in Southern
California. Basset, Male. Old Dog.
Wearing Outdated Tags.

The flyer gave a Nevada telephone number, and I made a note to check our local shelter on my next visit.

There was only one piece of personal mail, and I knew the scented parchment envelope was from Evie before I even looked at the San Diego return address. It was an invitation to a dinner party she and Howard were giving for Senator somebody or other. At the bottom of the cream inlaid card she had written: *Dee: I shan't take no for an answer. There will be some* Really Nice Men—(underlined!)—*most eligible. You can take your pick.* I could almost hear her clipped upper-crust English accent articulating the words.

That settled it. I wouldn't be going. Nothing was more off-putting than to be told you would be paraded before a lineup of what she considered to be RNM to whom, I was sure, she had already extolled my virtues, real and imagined. It would be embarrassing in the extreme. If she had calculated on a way to guarantee my refusal, she couldn't have chosen her words better.

But I had to admit, Evie, in her own odd way, only had my best interests at heart. Our long-standing friendship, begun as schoolgirls, entitled her to more consideration than I might otherwise have extended. Though her aristocratic background was so very different from my own, our friendship had endured through our extensive travels, travels which had ended somewhat abruptly when, soon after arriving in America, she'd been swept off her feet by Howard, a handsome and extremely wealthy Texas oilman. Had survived even after I, on one of the few impulses I have ever acted upon, and almost immediately regretted, married an associate of Howard's, who, though handsome and dashing, turned out on further acquaintance to be neither wealthy nor particularly trustworthy. The fact that he met with an untimely end not long after was, in Evie's opinion, which she seldom failed to express, "all for the best." Ever since then she had focused with singular intensity on finding the perfect RNM for me.

I went into the smaller of the two bedrooms, which served as both office and guest room, to check the answering machine and to listen again to the message that had been left the previous evening.

Beep: "Hello, Delilah. It's Beryl Handley. I don't know if you remember me. You gave me a little Shih Tzu last year? Don't worry, he's fine," she added, hurriedly, "But I do need your help. My parrot has been stolen—I think. No, I'm sure, stolen because her wings are clipped, so she couldn't have flown away."

I must admit I'd been procrastinating about returning the call, reluctant to take on what I was afraid would

turn out to be a hopeless case, yet not wanting to refuse
to help. But at the mention of the Shih Tzu I recalled
how kind Beryl had been to adopt him. The morning's
events had delayed my decision long enough. I picked
up the phone and dialed her number. I got the answering
machine and left a message to the effect that I would be
there first thing in the morning, and that she should call
me back if that wasn't convenient.

I was committed.

· 7 ·

The Client

"DO YOU REMEMBER the Shih Tzu?" Beryl Handley had said.

How could I forget? Though the day the little dog appeared on my doorstep (left, perhaps, by someone who knew of my interest in animals but preferred to remain anonymous), I couldn't tell what he was—a small bundle of black-and-grey matted fur, loaded with ticks, fleas, and foxtails; blind in one eye; ears so swollen with infection they stood out from his head. Starving, he had weighed less than seven pounds—the average for a Shih Tzu is around twelve.

Thinking the foundling might have been lost, or stolen and then abandoned, I had checked and rechecked my lost-and-found ads statewide, going back several months, but to no avail.

Dr. Willie, my local vet, had worked wonders restoring the little dog to health, but when the time came to take him home, he suggested instead that I consider giving him to a client of his, an older woman whose own Shih Tzu had recently died. After meeting Beryl, a lonely widow, I decided that these two needed each other, and little Saki, as he was to be named, was able to live out his remaining years in comfort and love.

"He was one of the lucky ones," I said to Watson as I drove my old Ford Country Squire north on PCH to Beryl's home in the small community of Sunset Beach. "How many more are out there, lost or abandoned, hiding in the bushes, too scared to come out and seek help?"

It was too sad to contemplate, and Watson made no reply other than to cozy up closer to me on the wagon's bench seat, as if to reassure me that she, at least, would never run away.

"Good girl," I murmured.

Beryl Handley lived in a ground-floor apartment in a complex occupied almost exclusively by senior citizens. She was pruning roses on the front patio when I arrived, her tiny frame standing on tiptoe to reach the topmost branches of a crimson climber.

"Delilah. How kind of you to come," she said, laying down the shears and taking off her gardening gloves to give me a hug. "Though I don't know how much you'll be able to help. I'm afraid I waited too long before calling you."

Saki, who had been lazing on a blanket nearby, opened his good eye and got up to greet Watson. After the obligatory sniffs had been exchanged, Watson joined the little dog, now plump and healthy, his coat shining, on the blanket.

"And you brought dear Watson with you," the old lady continued. "Would she like a drink?" Without waiting for a reply, she filled a bowl with water from a garden hose and placed it within Watson's reach.

"They're such a comfort, aren't they?" she said, looking at the two dogs. "I declare, if it wasn't for my little Saki, some mornings I'd have no reason to get out of bed. But Saki keeps me active, and he looks forward to his ride along the beach bike path every afternoon." She motioned toward an adult tricycle, with a basket attached to the front handlebars. "I don't care to drive much anymore," she added. "But most of the time the trike gets me where I want to go. And it's good exercise, too."

I had to admire this woman with her positive attitude toward the limitations of age, enjoying life where she could, finding compensations for the things she could no longer enjoy. I really hoped I'd be able to find her parrot for her.

Wiping her hands down her floral print pinafore, she continued, "Now, how about some lemonade? I just made it fresh from lemons in the backyard. Or, being English, perhaps you'd prefer tea?"

Having experienced a few too many cups of what passed for tea in America—hot water poured onto a tea bag of dubious herbal content—I said fresh-made lemonade sounded perfect.

Beryl led the way through the sliding glass doorway into a small living room. In one corner stood an empty dome-shaped metal cage giving mute and forlorn testimony to the missing runaway, or perhaps flyaway, would be more precise.

I took a closer look at the cage while Beryl went to the kitchen. Seed scattered on its floor was normal, but what was curious was the extraordinary number of red, yellow, and blue feathers, both in the cage and on the carpet. Clearly the bird had not left without a struggle.

The clink of ice cubes heralded Beryl's return from the kitchen. She was carrying a tray on which stood a large round pitcher of lemonade, condensation running down the sides, and two glasses. She held the tray unsteadily and I took it from her while we returned to the patio, setting it on a wrought-iron-and-glass table shaded by a huge green umbrella. Beryl poured the lemonade, and we settled down comfortably on chintz-covered cushions in wide redwood armchairs. The air was redolent with the scent of roses, mingled with a hint of salt spray from the nearby ocean. The distant buzz of traffic along PCH had an almost hypnotic effect, and I began to feel a little too relaxed, and had to remind myself I was there on business.

Beryl spoke first. "Now, before we start, you must tell me how much you charge for this kind of thing."

Like many seniors, she was living on a fixed income, and I hesitated to tell her of my usual rates—seventy-five dollars a day, plus expenses. I looked at Saki, dozing on the blanket alongside Watson, and thought of how fortunate I'd been to place him in such a loving home. That was reward enough.

"Let's see if I can help you first," I said. "If I'm successful you can have me and Watson over to dinner sometime." That alone would be worth the effort. I seldom cooked for myself, and Beryl was a talented chef— a regular prizewinner at the county fair.

Beryl looked doubtful. "Well, if you're sure . . ."

"I'm sure. Now tell me about your parrot. When did you discover it was gone?"

"Last Friday morning."

That would have been four days ago, I thought. The trail would already be cold.

"I covered her up as usual the night before when I went to bed," Beryl continued. "When I got up the next morning, the cover was still on the cage, but I thought it was funny that she wasn't fussing to get out. I was

afraid she was ill. But when I took the cover off..."
Tears filled her eyes as she relived the moment of dis-
covering her pet bird missing. "I realize now that I
should have called you sooner, but quite honestly it only
occurred to me yesterday there was anything that could
be done."

I leaned across and patted her arm. "Don't give up
hope. I can't make any promises, but I've brought many
pets home when their owners had thought they'd never
see them again." I omitted saying that this was my first
lost-bird case. "You said on the phone that her wings
were clipped. When was that? Couldn't they have grown
out?"

"Oh, no. I clip her wings regularly. Vance showed me
how."

"Vance?"

"Vance DeVayne, the man I got her from."

I got up and looked around for evidence of forced
entry. "Was there any sign of a break-in, through the
window, or the front door?"

"No. Not that I noticed. But I'm afraid I've been careless about the sliding glass door. The latch doesn't work
right, and I've been meaning to get it fixed."

I tried the door. It slid easily enough on its runner,
but the latch was broken, making it impossible to lock.

"Wouldn't Saki have alerted you to an intruder?"

She smiled wanly. "Neither of us heard a thing. But
you know we're both a little deaf, and once we're asleep,
it would take more than the door sliding open to wake
us."

"Has anybody, one of your neighbours, for instance,
admired the bird, perhaps to the point of wanting to take
it?" I hesitated to use the word "steal" in reference to
her neighbours.

"No. In fact, she's so noisy, has quite a vocabulary, you know, people wonder how I can stand it. But it's usually only first thing in the morning when she wakes up and wants attention."

I smiled. "What does she say?"

"She knows our names, my late husband Floyd's and mine. And a few bad words Floyd taught her." She smiled at the recollection, a sweet saucy smile that must have won Floyd's heart so long ago. "Oh, and she can bark like a dog. She got that from Saki. She can say his name, too, of course. They've become great friends. She calls out for Saki every morning first thing. That was the first hint I had that something was wrong. When she didn't call 'Saki, Saki.' "

At the sound of his name, the little Shih Tzu got up and came over to her. She picked him up and held him in her lap. Watson raised her head to see what was going on, then dropped it back on the blanket again.

"Perhaps someone objected to the noise, and maybe took her in desperation," I said. "Has anyone complained?"

That thought had obviously not occurred to her before, and she started to say something, then hesitated.

"What is it?" I encouraged.

"Well, Mr. Appleton, in 7-C, he's complained before. Old Crabby Appleton I call him," she said, her eyes twinkling. "But I don't think he'd go so far as to steal her."

"I'll have a quiet word with him, anyway," I said, adding, as she looked uncomfortable about approaching her neighbours about the bird's disappearance, "Don't worry. I'll just suggest he may have seen something that might help us find the bird.

"And you'd better give me a description of your parrot," I continued. I had no recollection of seeing a bird when I had originally delivered Saki to her, but it had been evening, and the bird may already have been covered.

"She's not really a parrot, she's a macaw. I say parrot because people don't always know what a macaw is. Her name is Scarlett. Scarlett O'Hara McCaw."

"So it's a female?"

"Vance thought so. It's not easy to tell with birds unless you have them checked by a vet. And we didn't want to pay the extra for that. It wasn't important. We didn't plan to breed her."

"Do you have a picture?"

Still carrying Saki, she went back into the living room and brought out a copy of *Bird Talk* magazine, on the cover of which were two magnificent birds, one blue and gold, the other predominantly red, with yellow and blue wing feathers.

"Scarlett looks just like this," she said, pointing to the red bird. "See the long tail feathers? Parrots have short tails."

Easy enough to distinguish a parrot from a macaw, then. But within their species birds have few, if any, distinguishing marks. Once they reached maturity one scarlet macaw would look very much like another, at least to the untutored eye. I would have my work cut out for me.

There was one hope. "Does Scarlett have any identification—a leg band, or a microchip?" I asked.

Beryl shook her head.

"How long have you had her?"

"Ten years. Since she was a baby. We hand-raised

her. She's very tame. They live for a hundred years or more, you know. I was sure she would outlast me, but now . . ." The tears returned.

"And you got her from, what was his name again? Vance?"

"Vance DeVayne. He owns Sweet Tweets, the bird farm in Surf City. He knows all about birds. He gave us a lot of help when we first got her. And I still get my supplies there—feed and vitamins."

Thinking it might be a case of birdnapping, I asked. "You've received no ransom note, or a phone call?"

"Oh my." She put the palm of a hand against her cheek. "You don't believe it could be anything like that, do you?"

"I don't believe anything at all. I'm just covering all possibilities."

"My dear, you're such a smart girl. I wish I had thought to call you sooner."

I smiled at the notion of being thought a girl by someone. "Is there anyone else who might have admired Scarlett, had access to your apartment, maybe, and taken it into their head to steal her?"

"Like who, do you mean?"

"A regular visitor, a janitor, the mailman, meter man, a gardener?"

"Well, there's José. But he wouldn't take Scarlett! He's so helpful and kind. He helps me with odd jobs sometimes. In fact, when he was here last I asked him to fix the lock on the sliding glass door. He said next time he came he'd bring a new fitting."

"José?" I said. "Where can I find him?"

"I don't know where he lives." She frowned. "I think he might be an illegal, you know. He comes and he goes.

He does odd jobs, and I pay him in cash."

"How did you meet him?"

"It was at Sweet Tweets. He was working for Vance. Last winter when my arthritis was so bad I couldn't get out he delivered some birdseed. Vance was so kind, sent him right over. After that, José got into the habit of stopping by from time to time to see if I had anything that needed doing."

I returned to the living room to take another look at the cage, and noticed a small stain, possibly blood, on the paper lining. Was it the thief's or the bird's? Scarlett hadn't gone without a struggle.

I pictured how it must have been. The beautiful red bird asleep on her perch, head tucked under her wing. One eye flickers open as she hears the glass door slide slowly on its runner. The thief steps inside the living room, pausing briefly to listen before warily crossing the room to the cage. Carefully the cover is removed, but before Scarlett has time to squawk, a gloved hand grabs her bony beak—there had to be gloves, those beaks and claws in the picture looked like they could inflict real damage. She's shoved into a carrier and spirited away— but not before someone sheds blood. There must have been a carrier of some sort, possibly tape for the beak. The thief wouldn't have walked through the apartment complex openly carrying a struggling, noisy bird.

Before I left the apartment complex I knocked on the door of apartment 7-C to have a word with Mr. Appleton, the neighbour Beryl thought might have a grudge against the noisy bird. He looked to be in his late seventies, and had been cautious about opening the door to a stranger.

"Pet detective, eh?" he said, looking at the card I handed through the barely opened door. "What'll they think of next?"

It turned out he had indeed seen José with the macaw a few days earlier. "Last Thursday, it was."

"What time was that?"

"Late in the evening, about ten. I thought I heard something, and looked out the window. I was going to call the police, but then I saw it was that guy José who helps some of the women around here with odd jobs."

"It was dark. How can you be so sure?"

"This place is well lit at night. Lights all along the pathway to the street."

"And you're sure he took the bird? You saw it?"

"Didn't exactly see it, no. But I could hear it squawking. It must have been in the bag he was carrying."

I was right. The thief had come prepared. I guessed this wasn't his first attempt at bird theft. "And you're positive it was José?"

"Sure. I didn't like the idea of him hanging around here after sundown, and I watched till he took off in that old blue pickup of his."

I sighed in annoyance. "Why didn't you tell Mrs. Handley?"

"It ain't none of my business. For all I knew she gave it to him. Good riddance, too. Noisy son of a gun, squawking all day long."

Beryl was right. Crabby is a good name for him, I thought as I made my way back to the car.

"Well, at least now we know for sure we're dealing with a theft, not a flyaway," I said to Watson as we drove off. "That improves our odds of bringing the missing macaw home. The first thing we have to do is to have a chat with this José, if we can find him. I think we'd better start by paying a visit to Mr. Vance De-Vayne of Sweet Tweets."

❖ 8 ❖

Sweet Tweets

THE SURF CITY pier was in view all the way as I drove back along PCH to Magnolia Street, where I would turn inland to the bird farm. The weather had warmed up, and the sun was shining, bringing people out to walk their dogs, play volleyball, sunbathe, or introduce their children to the joys of the waves. It was a different scene altogether to when I had discovered the body yesterday.

The morning's *Times* had carried the report, which said in part:

A local resident spotted the body at approximately 7:30 A.M. lying facedown at the water's edge under the Surf City pier. The victim is described as probably Latino, in his late twenties to early thirties. His height and weight were said by police to be approximately five feet eleven inches and 180 pounds. His hair was long, possibly worn in a ponytail. An autopsy was planned today to determine the cause of death, according to Surf City Police Lieutenant Jack Mallory.

He'll soon get to the bottom of it, I thought. Though our brief acquaintance had been fraught with misunder-

standings, despite our differences I had come to respect
Mallory, and to acknowledge his ability and intelligence
as a first-rate detective.

A police sketch accompanied the newspaper report,
which concluded with a request for anyone with information to call the county coroner's office or the Surf
City Police Department.

SWEET TWEETS WAS located about four miles inland,
between a strawberry field and an orange grove, in an
agricultural area gradually being overtaken by houses
and minimalls. But if it was possible to ignore the en-
croaching suburbia, one could almost imagine oneself
back in prewar Southern California.

A simple wooden sign illustrated with a cartoon bird
whistling music notes, and announcing SWEET TWEETS,
told me I'd found the right place. I parked my car in a
lot dominated by a two-storey grey clapboard building
which looked like it might be a restored farmhouse. The
ground floor had been renovated for business purposes,
and I guessed that the upper floor housed living quarters.
Beyond a chain-link gate at the side of the building I
could see several flight cages from which came the
squawking of many parrots.

I entered a store stocked with everything that could
possibly be required for a pet bird's comfort or its
owner's convenience. Elaborate cages, costing almost as
much as some of the birds they were intended to house,
were stacked along one wall, while another held bins of
feed—sunflower and safflower seeds, peanuts, millet
sprays, fruit-and-honey treats. One side of a centre island
displayed wooden nesting boxes of various designs,
along with plastic eggs (five for a dollar), presumably
intended to suggest to a bird what was expected of her

in the unlikely event she had forgotten. The other side held tapes and CDs for speech and song training (*Make Your Bird a Star*), toys—beads, mirrors, bells, swings, ropes—and books on the care and training of parrots, conures, macaws, budgerigars, canaries, cockatiels, and cockatoos, including the intriguing *How to Potty Train Your Bird in Fourteen Days.*

A dozen or so canaries trilled in chorus from cages behind the counter where a man was finishing serving a woman customer, packing seed, toys, and a book, *Care of Your Sun Conure,* into a plastic shopping bag, while she gazed with a mixture of apprehension and delight at the cage and the gorgeous yellow-and-orange bird it contained.

The man held the door open for her. "Give me a call anytime if you have questions," he said. "She'll be quiet for a few days while she gets used to her new surroundings, but she'll eat. Keep the cage out of drafts and cover her up in the evening. They like to go to sleep when the sun goes down, just like the wild birds do. Good luck!"

When she'd gone, he turned his attention to me. "How can I help you?"

I gestured to Watson, standing close by my side on a short leash. "Is it all right to bring the dog in?"

"As long as she doesn't bark and scare the birds," he said, petting Watson's head. "You can't leave her in your car; it's too hot."

I liked him already. With a ready smile in a round, apple-cheeked face, fair-skinned, with slightly receding reddish-blond hair curling closely to his head, he had a Celtic look about him, of Irish or Welsh extraction, perhaps. Short but sturdy. His rolled-up shirtsleeves displayed muscular arms.

"I'm looking for Mr. DeVayne," I said.

"You've found him."

"Oh, I thought . . ." I hesitated. "Excuse me, the way Mrs. Handley spoke, I expected you to be older."

"Mrs. Handley sent you? She must have been thinking of my dad. He died last year. I run the business now. I'm Vance Junior. Mrs. Handley usually phones in her order, so she probably hasn't heard about my dad. How is she? And how's the macaw? She dotes on that bird."

"Well, that's why I'm here. The bird is lost, and I'm rather afraid it's been stolen."

Vance frowned. "Stolen? Wow. Sorry to hear that."

I handed him my card. "Mrs. Handley hired me to find Scarlett, but I'm not sure there's much I can do."

He studied the card. "Pet detective, hmm. How can I help?"

He was one of the few people I'd met in the course of my work who didn't make some wisecrack about my profession. I appreciated his good manners.

"For a start, can you explain why anyone would want to steal a pet bird? Surely it wouldn't have much value."

"Don't you believe it. There's a big demand for stolen and smuggled birds since the feds passed a law banning the import of wild-caught exotics."

I was surprised. "I'd heard about the law, but I must confess I hadn't give much thought about what the consequences might be."

"Sure. Exotics can fetch as much as ten thousand dollars if you match the right bird with the right buyer."

"Really! I had no idea they were so valuable," I said.

"Yup. Ounce for ounce, parrots and other exotics can be worth more than cocaine."

This put a whole new light on the case, and I felt a tremor of apprehension as I realized who and what I might be dealing with.

Vance warmed to the subject. "There're also more and more birds being stolen with the intention of collecting a reward."

"Yes. That possibility had occurred to me. But so far Mrs. Handley hasn't received any phone call or ransom note."

"Then there's these self-described parrot rescue operations," he continued, obviously delighted to find a receptive ear. "They steal birds, or get difficult birds free from owners anxious to unload them, then sell them to a clueless buyer for a so-called adoption fee."

I felt overwhelmed. I hadn't realized the proportions of the problem. "Now I'm really baffled," I said. "I don't know where to start. What do you suggest?"

"Mrs. Handley should watch the classified ads, to see if anyone is offering a 'rescued' scarlet macaw for adoption," Vance said. "Or maybe she'll have someone contact her for a reward if she runs an ad."

Of course, I would place the ad myself. If some unscrupulous person should call seeking a reward, I could deal with them better than Beryl.

Vance tucked my card into his shirt pocket. "I'll keep my eyes and ears open and give you a call if I hear anything," he said.

Our conversation was interrupted by a light feminine voice teasing, "Are you boring the customer with your soapbox again, Vanny?" and a young woman entered the store from a back room.

Vance introduced her as his kid sister, Vera. The family resemblance was unmistakable. Short like him, but soft where he was stocky. The same reddish-blond hair curled attractively around face and ears, then fell in a plait down her back. She was wearing a long denim dress embroidered on the yoke with flowers and birds.

In one arm she cradled what she told me was a yellow-crested cockatoo. She scratched its head, and the bird closed its eyes in obvious bliss.

Vera turned to her brother. "If you want to show Mrs. Doolittle around, I'll watch the store."

"A tour would be nice, but actually, I was hoping to speak to José," I said. "Is he around? I understand he works for you. Mrs. Handley mentioned that he'd been doing some odd jobs for her recently. I thought he might know something about the missing bird." I was careful not to mention that José was already on my very short list of suspects.

At the mention of José, a blush crept over Vera's face, she put her hand to her neck, then, first placing the cockatoo on a T-stand beside the counter, she turned to busy herself rearranging stock on the centre island.

Her brother's face took on a guarded look. "José doesn't work here anymore," he said.

"That's too bad. Do you know how I might get in touch with him?"

"No, I don't. I have no idea where he went." Vance shrugged. "Maybe back to Mexico. I believe he has relatives in Tijuana."

I had obviously stumbled onto a sensitive situation. But I thought it best not to pry. I didn't want to run the risk of offending Vance or his sister. There was more than one way of eliciting information, and I needed to learn a lot more about the exotic-bird trade.

"Never mind," I said. "But I'd still like to take that tour, if you have the time."

At the change of subject, Vance recovered his good humour, opened the rear door, and led me out to the aviaries.

We walked down a path on either side of which were

cages large enough to allow the birds to fly freely.

A pair of magnificent birds of a deep cobalt blue soon caught my attention. These were Hyacinths, the largest of the macaws, Vance explained.

"Don't put your fingers in the cage," he warned as I stepped forward for a closer look. "That beak can crack a Brazil nut."

A breeding pair, they were the most expensive birds in the place, he said. "That's why they're here, close to the house, so I can keep an eye on them. Three times in the past twelve months birds have been snatched right off their perches, practically under our noses. That's more stolen birds in a year than in all the previous twenty-five years we've been in operation."

"Don't you have some kind of security system?" I asked.

"We're looking into it now. The thing is, it's never been necessary until recently. Sometimes, though, high value can protect birds from theft. A breeding pair like this, for instance, goes for thirty thousand dollars. Someone trying to sell a pair for less would be conspicuous."

He continued talking as we walked on down the aisle, passing cages of brilliantly coloured parrots, conures, macaws, and the smaller parakeets and cockatiels, finally stopping at a cage housing a forlorn-looking bird with a broken beak.

"At the other end of the scale, when things go wrong, birds are abandoned because they're sick, or the owner dies, or gets a divorce, a new baby, a new home—"

"The same reasons people give when they abandon dogs and cats," I put in.

Vance nodded. "People bring them here thinking they're giving me a deal. They're lucky I take them off their hands. I only do it for the birds. Some arrive with physical handicaps, like this redheaded Amazon, or because they don't get along with other pets."

"I'll tell you the most heartbreaking thing," Vance continued. "That's the birds nobody wants anymore. It's not any fault of theirs that they're at the mercy of people who never should have had the privilege of owning them in the first place. Birds are highly intelligent and social. They live a long time, and can get real attached to their owners. So if they outlive them . . ." He put up his hands in a gesture of hopelessness.

I thought of Beryl Handley. What would happen to Scarlett when she passed away? I hoped she'd made some kind of provision for her in her will. Of course, the point would be moot if I didn't find the bird.

"I can see I came to the right place," I said warmly. "Mrs. Handley was right. You really do know all about birds."

He smiled at the compliment. "This is what I do. It's my hobby as well as my living. I don't go to bars, I don't go to baseball games. I take care of my birds. It's a full-time job if you do it right. But I don't get too attached to them. Like I keep telling Vera—they're not family, they're stock."

I told him of my concern about being able to identify Scarlett if I did manage to track her down. "They all look the same," I said. "Even the males and females are not much different, right?"

He nodded in agreement. "That's right. Though female macaws are usually smaller. But sexing exotics is guesswork unless it's done by a vet, and that gets expensive. We usually only do it if the customer plans on breeding."

We were making our way back when, through the chain-link gate, I saw a police car pull into the parking lot, and was disquieted to see Detective Mallory and Sergeant Offley get out and head toward the store. Adding to my discomfort was the tiny thrill of pleasure I felt at seeing Mallory again. Pleasure, I was quite sure, he would not share on finding me here. Whatever *his* reason for being at the bird farm, I knew he would not approve of *mine*. But any hope I might have had of making my escape unnoticed was dashed as Mallory paused and looked at my station wagon, his gaze traveling from the Union Jack decal on the bumper to myself standing with Vance and Watson just a few feet from the gate.

9

Crossed Paths and Purposes

VERA CAME DOWN the path toward us. Her fair complexion shaded from the sun by a wide-brimmed hat, she made an enchanting picture.

"There's a policeman here, asking for you," she said to her brother.

But Vance had seen the police car at the same time as I did, and was already heading back to the store.

Vera and I followed at a more leisurely pace. I had opted to accompany her, not wanting to leave and have Detective Mallory think I was avoiding him. Anyway, I had to admit, I was curious.

"Do you know what that's all about?" I asked.

A frown appeared between her delicately shaped eyebrows. "Something to do with José, the man who used to work here," she said. "I thought that business was over and done with."

What business? I wondered.

We entered the store in time to hear Vance saying to Offley, "Hey, if it's about that bogus green card of his, I took it in good faith. I hired him as a day labourer."

Day labourer. I had seen the Mexican immigrants, legal—and otherwise, I'd heard—sitting on the curb along

Main Street, hoping to find work. Employers, often land-scape gardeners or building contractors looking for casual workers, would cruise by in their trucks, call out what the job was, and one or more men would jump into the truck bed. I don't know the legal merits of the practice, but it seemed to work well enough: small businesses had access to cheap labour, while otherwise unemployable, perhaps undocumented workers had the opportunity of gainful employment.

Possibly Vance had run into trouble in this regard.

Offley blew out his cheeks. "Card was a fake, easy enough to spot," he said, apparently anxious to establish his credentials as a well-informed lawman. With those jowls of his and a permanently doleful expression in his droopy eyes, he looked for all the world rather like a bad-tempered Basset hound.

Mallory, who had been watching the cockatoo preen itself, looked up at me, showing no surprise at my presence. I nodded. "Good morning, Mrs. Doolittle," was his only acknowledgment. Wearing a grey worsted suit, maroon shirt, and lighter maroon tie, he looked more like he was dressed for the racetrack owner's enclosure than for official business. I wondered, not for the first time, how he could afford to dress so well on a policeman's salary.

He now took over the interview from Offley, saying to Vance, "We have it on record that he filed an assault complaint against you."

Vance looked disgruntled. "He dropped the charges," he said. "He knew he'd asked for it."

"What was the dispute about?" said Mallory.

"It's in the record," said Vance sullenly.

"Humour me," said the detective.

"I caught him stealing fledglings. I'd had my suspicions after some eggs disappeared, but when the fledglings were missing, I knew it had to be him. He was always in here asking questions about sales and the value of various birds when he should have been outside cleaning cages."

"Why would anyone steal eggs?" asked Mallory.

"Money. What else?" Vance shrugged. "It's profitable, raising young parrots from eggs instead of allowing them to be hatched and weaned by their parents. It makes my blood boil. Not a week goes by that we don't see birds maimed by incorrect handling after birth."

Vera gently touched his arm in an attempt to calm him, but he shook her off angrily. Then, perhaps realizing he'd said too much, he managed a grim smile, and asked, "What's all this about, anyway?"

"We're investigating the death of José Martinez, a drowning victim," said Mallory. "We found evidence in his vehicle that he was a former employee of yours. We've made a tentative ID of the body, pending confirmation by the victim's family, but we're ninety-nine percent sure that it's Martinez."

So it was José Martinez whose body I'd found on the beach. The shock of that information soon gave way to dismay at the realization that my one and only lead to the missing macaw was dead.

Vera put her hand to her throat. "Poor José. How sad," she said.

"What's that got to do with us?" asked Vance. "An unfortunate accident."

"It was no accident," said Offley officiously. "The coroner's examination shows he was dead before he entered the water."

Vance's expression changed from one of near indif-

ference to an accidental drowning of someone whom he
obviously disliked, to one of alarm.

"I hope you don't think I had anything to do with it,"
he declared hotly.

I didn't think for a moment that Vance was guilty of
anything other than perhaps a certain rashness in defense
of his birds. But he wasn't helping his case by his belligerent attitude.

"The case is still under investigation," said Mallory.
"Since no one knows exactly how long Martinez was in
the water, it's difficult to pinpoint the exact time of
death. Right now everyone who's had contact with him
in the past couple of weeks is a suspect. We're following
all possible leads. We may need to contact you again
for details of your recent activities. I hope you'll make
yourself available."

In other words, don't leave town, I thought grimly.

Mallory turned to Vera. "How about you? Have you
seen or heard from Martinez lately?"

Vance pushed himself in front his sister. "See here.
She's got nothing to do with this," he said, raising his
voice.

Vera touched his arm gently. "It's all right, Vanny.
The detective's only doing his job." Then turning to
Mallory, she said, "I haven't seen José since he quit
working here." Her voice was calm, but I could tell she
was flustered from the way she lowered her eyes after
speaking and fidgeted with the plait falling forward over
her shoulder. But then, who wouldn't be nervous in such
circumstances?

With a reassuring smile at Vera, the detective closed
his notebook, indicating the interview was at an end.

I had no reason to linger, either. I had found out as
much as I could about scarlet macaws, more than I had

anticipated about the illegal traffic in exotic birds, and certainly more than I had expected about José. It seemed more than likely that, among other "odd jobs," José had stolen Scarlett O'Hara, and sometime afterward had come to a bad end. Where did that leave Scarlett?

Gone with the wind, no doubt.

Either she'd escaped and flown away, in which case she could be anywhere by now. Or some other person, possibly José's killer, now had possession of her. Since her wings were clipped, the latter was the more likely scenario. In that case, I still had a chance, however remote, of finding her. But which way to turn? At the moment it seemed my best option would be to stay closely in touch with Detective Mallory.

We left the bird farm at the same time. In the parking lot I did not immediately hurry to my car, as I might otherwise have done, but made myself available for the inevitable question. It was not long in coming.

"What brings you here, Mrs. Doolittle?" asked the detective.

I bit my tongue on any tart reply that otherwise might have presented itself, and said, "Pure coincidence, I assure you. My client, Mrs. Beryl Handley of Sunset Beach"—I made a point of giving him details in the hope that he wouldn't think I was making it up, and I could swear I saw an eyebrow raise imperceptibly in interest—"has hired me to find her valuable macaw, which I suspect has been stolen. Mrs. Handley mentioned that José had been doing odd jobs around her apartment complex, and had shown particular interest in the bird. And a neighbour of hers claims to have seen him take it. All Mrs. Handley could tell me about José's background was that he worked here. So here I am."

I paused for breath, then added, "How about yourself?

Oh, I know why you're here, but what was your lead?"

"We ask the questions, ma'am," put in Offley.

Not very promising, and I was turning to leave with an oh-well-I-tried shrug when Mallory said, "You say your client lives in Sunset Beach? That's where we found Martinez's pickup, illegally parked in a cul-de-sac. Evidence in the cab, including several red feathers, led us here."

It was all I could do to keep from reminding him of the red feather I'd pointed out on the victim's body at the beach.

"TONY WAS WRONG, then," I said to Watson as we made our way home. "It wasn't Little Bob's friend Joe whose body you found."

Watson looked at me; the brown dots over her eyebrows seemingly raised in question.

"What is it?" I asked. "You don't agree?"

We were waiting for the traffic signal at the corner of Magnolia and PCH. It was the dinner hour, and beachgoers, tourists, and commuters all seemed to have hit the highway at the same time.

"Hang on." I negotiated the tricky left turn back on to PCH, then said, "José—Spanish for Joseph, as in Joe? I say, Watson old girl, there's a clue here somewhere. Joe, José? Could they possibly be one and the same?"

. 10 .

The Game's Afoot

THE FOLLOWING MORNING I was studying the classifieds for a lead to Scarlett's disappearance, when, alerted by Watson to an approaching car, I became aware of the distinctive sound of Tony's vintage woody station wagon pulling into the driveway. This was soon followed by the flap of his rubber thongs along the path at the side of the house. Trixie, his Jack Russell terrier, preceded her master into the kitchen and promptly headed for Watson's food bowl. Watson, trying to be good, sent a puzzled look in my direction, and then stood politely by as her guest chomped down on the kibble.

"Morning, luv," said Tony, poking his head around the kitchen door. "Any chance of a cuppa?"

Like master, like dog, I thought to myself.

Although Tony's unannounced visits were never entirely welcome, I had to admit that his cheery presence was refreshing. His Cockney wit and bright outlook on life invariably gave me a lift.

I plugged in the electric kettle. "What's up?" I asked.

He sat down at the kitchen table, pulling out a crumpled envelope from the pocket of his black OP shorts as he did so. I recognized it immediately. It was identical to the one I had received containing Evie's invitation.

"I got this 'ere invite from yer mate Mrs. Cavendish," he said. "It's this Friday. Thought we could drive down together."

"I'm not going," I said.

"Not going? That's daft. She's yer best mate. C'mon luv. It'll do you good to get out. 'Ave a bit of a knees-up."

Tony's idea of a dinner party was obviously quite a bit different to Evie's, and indeed to mine. There would be no rowdy "Knees Up Mother Brown" dance—a favourite at Cockney gatherings—at Evie's soiree, as I tried to explain.

"Well, then, they need us there to brighten things up," he retorted. "Show 'em a thing or three."

Not bothering to argue the point, I offered him the tin of Cadbury's chocolate biscuits I had just taken out of the cupboard, and changed the subject.

"I've been wondering about that Joe person. You know, the friend of Bobbi and Little Bob who you thought might have been the drowning victim. What did he look like?"

"Youngish, late twenties. Mexican. Ponytail." He broke off a piece of his chocolate biscuit and gave it to Trixie. "Why? What's on your mind?"

I showed him the newspaper clipping with the police sketch of the victim.

"That's 'im all right," he said. "Joe, José. It's all the same difference." He pronounced both versions with a hard *J*. "Can't seem to get me tongue 'round the Spanish lingo."

Trixie jumped into his lap, mooching after the remainder of his biscuit. Tony scratched her absently behind the ear, then said again, "Why?"

"It's that case I've been working on, the stolen macaw, remember? It turns out that the thief might have been this same Joe, or José, whatever you want to call him."

"Wouldn't put it past 'im," said Tony dryly. " 'E was always on the twist, that one. Though I wouldn't 'ave thought nicking birds would've been worth the risk."

I told him about my visit to Sweet Tweets and what I had learned from Vance about the money to be made trading exotic birds.

"Get away," said Tony in astonishment.

"Yes. Parrots are the pet of the nineties. And when the law was passed prohibiting the import of wild-caught birds, it increased the incentive for smuggling and theft."

I poured myself another cup of tea, and held the teapot over Tony's cup in silent inquiry.

"Ta, luv," he said in reply. "Lovely cup of cha you make." Then he went on, "So you think that's why your client's bird was stolen?"

"It's possible. And," I said, pausing for effect, "who do you think I ran into at the bird farm?" Then, without giving him a chance to reply: "Detective Mallory! And you'll never guess what he said."

"He asked you out?"

"He did no such thing," I said, colouring. "Why ever would you say that?"

Tony tapped the side of his nose knowingly. "Plain as the nose on yer face," he said. "You two have the 'ots for each other."

"Nonsense," I said. "And there's no need to be so crude. What I was going to say was, this José"—I pointed at the police sketch—"used to work at Sweet

Tweets, and apparently filed an assault charge against the owner after he was caught stealing baby birds, and he and the owner had a bit of a dustup. Mallory was following up on leads. He told me they'd found José's pickup in Sunset Beach, right near where my client lives."

"So you think that after he stole the bird, someone did 'm in, then dunked 'im in the drink?"

"It seems likely," I said. "But that's Mallory's problem to get sorted. I'm only interested insofar as it affects me and my case."

"Hmm." Tony scratched his near-bald, tanned head. "Let me 'ave a bit of a think." He was sharp as a tack, and for a man in his seventies, in remarkably good physical shape. Though, as he often joked, "In dog years I'm dead."

His eyes lit up, in apparent inspiration. "You know me mate Slippery? 'Im with the snakes?"

I nodded, recalling Slippery Sam Vyper, a reptile collector who had played a role in an earlier case of mine—the Careless Coyote Affair, the press had dubbed it at the time.

"Well, some of his specimens are on the endangered list, and the only ones he can get 'is 'ands on are smuggled in across the Mexican border. 'E was telling me about this bloke in Tijuana who deals in all kinds of exotics. Bet 'e could give us a lead. I'll ask Slippery to see if he can get us a word wiv 'im." He spooned more sugar into his tea and stirred thoughtfully." In fact, if we was to go to Mrs. C's party, we could nip across to TJ while we was down there, San Diego being so close to the border an' all. Kill two birds with one stone, like." His eyes twinkled at the pun.

Considering the object of my quest, I was not thrilled with the analogy, but conceded he had a point. I found myself wavering. Perhaps I did owe it to Evie to attend the party which was so important to her. And I certainly needed to follow up all possible leads in my search for Scarlett.

"Come on, luv," Tony was saying.

"All right," I agreed reluctantly.

"Brilliant. Mission accomplished," he said, smiling. He tucked the invitation back in his pocket and prepared to leave.

"But you'd better behave yourself," I admonished.

The words were wasted. With Trixie at his heels he was already heading out the back door, promising to ring me later when he had set up an appointment with our TJ connection.

Behave yourself. I had not chosen the words lightly. Though Tony insisted that he had retired from his life of crime, he had been known to backslide occasionally. "But," he would insist, when pressed, "only in a small way." Whatever that may mean. I tolerated him out of loyalty to my late husband, whose colleague he had been, and also, I had to admit, because his compendium of crooks and murky acquaintances could sometimes prove useful in my work.

With some misgivings about the wild-goose chase I had possibly let myself in for, I returned to my classifieds. I was surprised at the number of exotic birds listed for sale: African greys, sun conures, Amazons, cockatoos. I was better able to visualize them all after my visit to Sweet Tweets. *Cockatoo,* read one, *18-months-old, hand fed, lovable, talks good, loves attention.* Only a few months into its one-hundred-year life span, and already looking for a new home. If it's so lovable, why did they want to get rid of it? Probably too noisy. Translate the "talks" into "screeches for attention" and we'd be closer to the truth. Of course it wants attention. Birds are social animals. No point getting one, leaving it alone all day, then expecting it to be silent when you got home.

Similar ads were repeated over and over. Birds, young, lovable, friendly, with cage, all furnishings included, going for around a thousand dollars. It was a new riff on the old disposable-pet syndrome, long a factor in the unwanted dog and cat problem.

Listed in amongst the more lowly doves and racing pigeons were three macaws: two blue and gold, one scarlet (*Cheap; talks; lots of fun!*). I circled the ad with my red marker pen. Maybe this was one of those birds stolen for a reward that Vance had told me about. I picked up the telephone and dialed the number.

But the pleasant woman who answered sounded genuine enough. Her mother had passed away recently, she told me, and there was no one else in the family interested in taking on the bird. "But it has to be the right home," she said earnestly. "That's why we're selling it cheap. We would insist on a home interview first. Have you had a parrot before?"

Disappointed, I made my excuses and got off the phone. But at least she was doing it right. I would never place a pet in a new home without an interview and a home visit. In its own way, pet placement is as big a responsibility as adopting a child.

I drafted my own ad for Scarlett O'Hara—*Lost; scarlet macaw. Vicinity Sunset Beach*—giving my telephone number and indicating a reward.

After I'd called in the ad to the newspaper, I checked for my outstanding lost-dog cases. Though some were several weeks old by now, I never gave up hope. There was always the chance that the pet might have been taken in by somebody, and would eventually get out again. "If it ran away from you, it can run away from them," I advised distraught owners who suspected their pet might have been stolen once it had escaped from the backyard. Then, too, people sometimes took in a stray out of the goodness of their hearts and then, after a few weeks, realized that it wasn't working out. Then they would advertise it, either as a "free to you" or a "found."

"Aha!" I said to Watson. "What's this?"

At the bottom of the lost-and-found column, a boxed announcement in bold type had caught my eye. The animal shelter was holding an auction of unclaimed exotic animals, including birds, reptiles, and potbellied pigs, the following day. Perhaps Scarlett O'Hara McCaw would be among the items offered. I wielded my red marker again. I would be at the auction early the next morning.

• 11 •
Sold!

"FIFTY. I HAVE fifty. Do I hear sixty? Two red-tailed boas, six feet in length. A breeding pair. Must go together."

Mike Denver, chief animal control officer at the shelter, announced the bidding while two kennel attendants displayed a sinewy reptile, its mottled, reddish-brown skin glistening in the afternoon sun.

I had not been prepared for the sad assortment of animals assembled at the shelter's monthly auction. Livestock, geese, chickens, turtles, snakes, iguanas, a potbellied pig, pet birds of all kinds—budgies, a cockatiel, various parrots—though no scarlet macaw, I soon noted. Everything but dogs and cats. From good homes and bad, caring and uncaring owners, they were here because their owners were either no longer able, or willing, to care for them.

The crowd was as varied as the animals. Farmers, ranchers, people drawn by compassion, or in hopes of finding a bargain. A man and a little girl, looking at a pony; a woman and her daughter, intent on bidding for the chickens and geese. I thought I recognized Slippery Sam, Tony's snake-collecting friend.

I read the cards attached to each pen, cage, or tank. The pony had been found wandering down a canyon roadway, never claimed, presumed abandoned. On the boas' tank the words "police hold" had been scratched out and "available" inserted. A possible indication that the owner was in jail and, being unlikely to be able to claim his property in the near future, had released it to the shelter. Two of the iguanas had been turned in when they got too large to handle and their owners had lost interest in them.

Like the one whose tank Mike was standing by now.

"Lot number thirty-seven. A ten-year-old iguana," his big voice boomed. "I'm opening the bidding at twenty dollars."

A scruffy-looking person raised his hand.

Mike nodded acknowledgment. "Twenty! Do I hear thirty?"

"Thirty!" I was aghast to hear myself utter. What in the world did I want with an iguana? I didn't even have a setup for it. I just felt sorry for it, and besides, I didn't like the look of the chap I was bidding against.

"Forty," he said.

I dropped out of the bidding when it reached one hundred, breathing a sigh of relief when a voice across from me called out "One hundred and ten!" It was Myra Shepperd, curator of the local zoo. While no fan of zoos in general, I knew that in Myra's capable hands the iguana would at least have a decent habitat and the correct diet.

The bidding for the cockatiel was desultory. Hardly surprising. The poor thing, a robin-sized grey and white bird, sat shivering in the bottom of the cage, its yellow crest drooping miserably. Its owner had died, and apparently no one in the family had been willing to take it on. How dismayed the owner would have been to see her pet in such reduced circumstances, I thought.

Mike was waiting for an opening bid. "Five dollars," I heard myself say. I was doing it again. Clearly I had no business attending an animal auction.

"Ten!" This from a woman behind me.

"Fifteen," I said.

"Twenty!"

I looked around to see who was bidding against me, and saw that it was Tony's neighbour Bobbi Briscoe. Maybe she planned to rehabilitate the bird to resell at a profit. Or perhaps she just wanted the cage; that alone was worth twenty dollars.

My dander was up. "Twenty-five," I said, determined that she wasn't going to put this unfortunate creature with the rest of her dismal flock.

I waited for her to offer thirty. But she knew as well as I did that the bird wasn't worth it, even with the cage thrown in.

Bobbi leaned over my shoulder. "You'll spend ten times that at the vet," she said, sneering. She was gone in a cloud of cheap perfume before I could think of a suitable rejoinder.

Before claiming my new pet, I made my customary systematic tour of the shelter, checking my notes as I went.

I stopped at the cage of an old Basset hound. With grizzled nose and coat faded and thinning with age, he looked at me mournfully through the cage bars. If Sergeant Offley had a dog, it would be a Basset, I decided, recalling my theory that over time pets and their owners start to resemble each other. The dog was sitting close to the gate; he had not yet given up hope that his owner would appear. He was wearing a tag and I knelt beside the cage, put my hand through the bars and petted him, and jotted down the information on the tag—an expired Nevada license. I remembered the flyer I'd received recently about a lost Basset. It had stated that the dog was wearing an outdated Nevada tag. I noted the cage number and went and stood in line at the kennel-office window.

"Next. Oh, hi, Delilah," said Rita, the office manager, looking up from completing her last transaction. "Mike told me you were here. What brings you in today?" Her bright, pretty face was always a welcome sight in this gloomy place. She paused to brush her blond bangs out of her eyes before taking the auction claim slip from me.

"Actually, I came for the auction," I said, fishing in my purse for the twenty-five dollars. "But I just noticed the Basset in cage fifty-seven. How long's he been here?"

California shelters are required by law to keep pets a minimum of seven working days if they have some form of ID, a mere three days if not. After that they are put up for adoption, and sadly, if no one wants them, they are eventually euthanized.

Rita's long sculpted nails tapped her computer keyboard. "He's already been here a week," she said. "Time's up tomorrow. He's so old there's not much chance he'll be adopted. We've tried to trace the tag, but it's long since expired and Nevada Animal Control has no record."

"I think I might have a line on the owner," I said eagerly. "Can you give him a reprieve while I get in touch?"

Rita made a note to hold the dog for three more days, then said, "I was going to call Basset Rescue before we made final disposition, but go ahead and check out your lead first."

Breed rescue groups do a wonderful job of taking in unwanted dogs and caring for them until they can find them new homes. I often refer people to them if they are unable to find what they want at the shelter.

On my way out to the parking lot I saw Slippery Sam. He didn't acknowledge my wave; he was too intent on backing his truck up to the gate where a kennel attendant waited with a trolley carrying the boa tank. Great! The boas had a good home. Whatever his shortcomings—and I gathered from Tony they were many—there was no question that Slippery dearly loved his snakes.

WATSON WAS EAGERLY awaiting me in the station wagon. Dog visitors are not allowed in the shelter; they're too much of a distraction to the inmates. And since there was always a chance she might pick up an infection or parasites, I was quite content to abide by the rules.

She was all waggy-tailed curiosity to see the cage and its occupant.

"Now, be nice, Watson," I said, covering the cage with a towel to protect the bird from being bewildered by its surroundings. "This poor birdie's been through a lot. We don't need to traumatize him or her any more than necessary."

Watson seemed to respect my concern. A shelter grad herself, she knew how confusing and insecure it was to be handed from one stranger to another, then another.

We stopped off at the pet store on the way home to buy seed, gravel, and a bird vitamin block. I didn't know exactly what else an ailing bird might need. I would take it to the vet in a day or so, and let Dr. Willie check it over. Or maybe my new acquaintance, Vance DeVayne, would be better able to advise me.

• • •

ARRIVING HOME, I set the cockatiel's cage on the kitchen counter until I could decide on a permanent location. When I opened the little door to survey how best to go about giving the cage a much-needed cleaning, the bird surprised me by hopping out onto my finger. From there it fluttered to the window ledge, where it pecked away at the cracker crumbs I put out for it, occasionally turning a little black eye in my direction to watch as I changed the paper lining the cage bottom, scrubbed the perches, put fresh food and water into the cleaned seed cups, and attached the vitamin block to the side of the cage.

After feeding Watson and Hobo, I decided I deserved a cup of tea for my efforts. I plugged in the electric teakettle, took the lid off the teapot, and set it aside with two of my favourite PG Tips tea bags. While waiting for the water to boil I went into the den to look for the lost-Basset flyer. The answering machine was blinking three calls. They would have to wait until after I'd had my tea. Contacting the Basset's owners took priority. I dialed the Nevada number, but apparently there was no one home, so I left a message on the answering machine to the effect that I might have located their dog, and that they should call me back as soon as possible.

When I returned to the kitchen the bird was gone! How stupid of me! I had forgotten to put it back in the cage and it must have flown away at the first opportunity. But all the doors and windows were closed: it had to be in the house somewhere.

For one horrible moment I thought that Hobo had finished it off, but the feral feline was still on the back porch eating his dinner. What about Watson? Had she surrendered to her baser animal instincts and snatched the bird? But she had followed me into the den.

Hearing a faint twitter, the first sound the bird had uttered since we left the shelter, I looked up to see if it was perching somewhere overhead, on the light fixture perhaps. A second chirp had me looking in the direction of the kitchen counter, the third led me to the uncovered teapot. There was the cockatiel, its yellow crest waving valiantly as it struggled to pull itself over the rim of the pot with its beak, unable to get a purchase on the smooth china. It couldn't fly out—the opening was too narrow.

I tried everything, first turning the teapot upside down to shake the bird out, then laying the pot on its side to enable it to walk out. Nothing worked.

The cockatiel was beginning to tire from the effort and I realized that I was faced with a tough decision. It was between the bird and the teapot—a choice no Englishwoman should have to make. With Watson watching my every move, I placed the teapot on the floor, covered it with blanket, then tapped gently with a hammer until I felt the pot break. A very bemused bird emerged from the wreckage, fluttered up to the counter and back into the now spotless cage, whereupon I quickly closed the door. Fluffing up its feathers with a satisfied chirp, the bird watched as I swept up the shards of my favourite teapot and dumped them in the trash bin under the sink. Not an auspicious beginning to our relationship.

"Talk about curiosity killing the cat!" I said to Watson. "The cat's got nothing on this featherbrain. Another minute or two and our cockatiel would have been bird soup."

Shaken, with not even a decent cup of tea to settle my nerves, I turned to studying the lost and found bird column in the classifieds. An ad for a found African grey caught my eye, and remembering what Vance had said about birds being kidnapped for ransom, out of curiosity I dialed the number.

"What's the reward?" a woman's raspy voice responded in answer to my inquiry.

There was no doubt to whom the voice belonged. I had already heard it once that day. It was my auction foe Bobbi Briscoe.

I hoped she didn't recognize my voice. I tried for an American accent, not entirely successfully, I'm sure.

"Reward? I'm a senior citizen on a fixed income. I'm afraid I can't afford very much." I tried to sound frail and elderly. "Please, can I come and see the bird?"

"No. It's not yours," she replied. "The owner picked it up this morning."

She was obviously holding out for a big reward. There was not much point in arguing. So I hung up, sure that she was lying; I knew for a fact she'd been at the shelter all morning. But I had no proof she had stolen the bird, and no way of going about getting any. I didn't even own an African grey. After all, I was lying, too.

It was an hour or so later before I got around to running back my messages.

Beep: "Hallo." It was a woman's voice. "My vet Dr. Scott gave me your number. He said you might be able to help me. There's a cat up in a tree across the street. It's been there three days. It keeps crying. I've called animal control and the fire department, but they won't do anything. Can you help?"

"Who do they think I am? Rescue central?" I said to Watson, dozing at my feet.

Nevertheless, I called back immediately and explained to a very agitated woman that official agencies rarely respond to such calls, citing liability concerns.

"They told me that the cat would come down when it

got hungry enough; they've never seen a dead cat in a tree," she said.

"Of course they haven't," I said indignantly. "That's because when the cat gets weak enough it will fall out of the tree, and if it's not dead when it hits the ground, it will crawl away to who knows what fate."

I advised her to call a tree trimmer. "You'll have to pay him, of course. Maybe other concerned neighbours will be willing to share the cost with you."

She thanked me profusely for this simple solution, and I was relieved that at least one problem that day was on its way to being taken care of.

The next call was not so likely to have a satisfactory outcome.

Beep: "A friend told me you go to the shelter a lot." I guessed the voice belonged to an older woman. "Do you know if anyone has turned in an injured rat?"

The message raised more questions than answers. Was it a pet rat that had been injured? In that case, how could she have lost track of it? If, on the other hand, it was a pesky rodent, then why did she care, other than having a desire to follow the hunter's code of always tracking and finishing off the prey? In the case of a rat, however, that seemed to be taking the humane ethic to extremes.

I called back and left a message on her machine asking for more information, but suggesting she visit the animal shelter herself.

The last call was from Tony, telling me that he had contacted his TJ connection, and we were to meet him the day after tomorrow, following Evie's party.

· 12 ·
Delilah Goes South

THE NEXT DAY, as we motored south on the 405 freeway to San Diego, I asked Tony, "How well do you know Bobbi Briscoe?"

"What d'you mean?"

I tried to choose my words carefully. I was unclear as to the nature of their relationship and I didn't wish to offend. But there was little tact in my question: "Is she a genuine bird rescuer, or is she just in it for the money?"

Tony wrinkled his face in wry contemplation. "Everyone's on the twist one way or another, luv," he said noncommittally.

"You speak for yourself," I said, adding with some asperity that whatever his cronies might get up to, my circle of acquaintance, present company excepted, was scrupulously honest.

"Nah, then," said Tony. "Don't get aerated. I only means as 'ow we all 'as to make a living as best we can, and where's the 'arm in a little graft 'ere and there?"

"I beg to differ," I said. "Rescuing genuinely lost or unwanted birds, rehabbing them, and trying to recoup the expense is one thing; stealing, causing grief to the owner, then holding out for a reward is an entirely different matter."

Decidedly put out, I turned my head and looked out the window. On the one side, surf, sand, and sailboats greeted the eye; on the other, rolling hills, green now from the winter rains, would soon give added meaning to California's motto "the Golden State."

We were in Tony's woody station wagon, Watson and Trixie in the back, smudging up the rear window with damp nose prints. Tony kept the engine well tuned, but the car rattled and squeaked at the slightest bump in the road, making it seem as if we were going much faster than the sixty-five-mile-per-hour limit. With a surfboard on the roof rack, I rather thought we must look a bit like the Ma and Pa Kettle of surfdom in search of the perfect wave on the fountain of youth.

"Take Slippery's mate Gomez," said Tony, continuing his train of thought.

"Gomez?"

"The bloke we're going to see tomorrow about them birds of your'n. According to Slippery, 'e's got a regular business in TJ, one of them souvenir shops. But when the lights are low "—Tony hesitated, checking his rear-view mirror as we merged with the I-5 traffic coming from Los Angeles and points north— "'e smuggles— birds, reptiles, lizards. Whatever you want, 'e can get 'is 'ands on it. Don't ask no questions, just pay the price and move on."

"But that's not right," I said. "There're good reasons why these animals aren't allowed in. Possible damage to local plants and animals, not to mention taking too many from their native habitat. Vance DeVayne says that four wild-caught birds die for every one who survives the transition to captivity."

"Cor, listen to you. 'Vance says, Vance says.' Carrying on alarming you are. I didn't say I liked it, I said that's the way it is. But I'm warning you. You won't get much information out of Gomez if you take that attitude. Best let me do the talking."

I wasn't sure that letting Tony do the talking would ever be best, but I let the matter drop for the moment.

"Any old 'ow, we're meeting 'im at the Big Boy restaurant tomorrow afternoon."

He seemed to know his way around the Mexican border town and I asked if he went there often.

"Regular like. Get me teeth fixed, me car painted and detailed. Get me prescriptions, too. They're a lot cheaper than in the States."

Hearing an unfamiliar rustle behind me, I turned around to see Trixie nibbling at my garment bag. "No, don't do that, sweetie," I said, giving her a gentle push. The bag contained my one good dinner dress, and I didn't want it covered in dog hair, or worse. The little terrier took the scolding well, circled a place on her blanket, and settled down for a nap.

"Dress optional" the invitation had said, indicating that anything from nakedness on up would be acceptable. I rather fancied myself in the long black jersey wool T-shirt–style dress. Though I wasn't totally sure the side slits were appropriate for someone my age, I thought the high neckline that dipped to a vee in back, and the long sleeves, had a very sophisticated look. I hoped that Evie would approve.

Dressing for the occasion in Southern California was always a trifle hazardous. One was more likely to be over-than underdressed. The British have a tradition of dressing for dinner even when on safari or during other strenuous expeditions, and I had never got used to the fact that in Southern California you could dress for the most formal-sounding evening and be greeted by a host in shorts and T-shirt and a hostess in fetching but wildly inappropriate workout tights, saying, "Oh, you shouldn't have bothered." One wonders how the Duchess of Windsor might have reacted to a "dress optional" invitation. Probably with as much dismay as a request to B.Y.O.B.

Tony didn't appear to have brought anything more than a change of jeans and T-shirts in his duffel bag. I hoped Evie wouldn't be offended that he didn't wear a suit. Probably not. She had a soft spot for Tony, and in her eyes the old reprobate could do no wrong.

I looked at my watch. It was already half-past four, and I was afraid we were going to be late. "Pimm's and nibbles at six," Evie had said. It was already four-thirty, commute time, and we had been late getting away. My fault. Tony had picked me up on time, but though I had remembered to leave food and water out for Hobo, and locked the doggie door to prevent him getting in after my new pet bird, when Tony arrived I was still dithering about where to leave the bird's cage while I was gone overnight. I finally settled on the table by the sitting-room window where the cockatiel could catch the morning rays and watch the wild birds splashing in the birdbath.

Tony saw me anxiously checking my watch. "Don't worry, luv. I'll 'ave us there in plenty of time."

• 13 •

Pimm's and Nibbles

TONY WAS RIGHT. Though a few minutes late, we were, nevertheless, the first to arrive. Appearing at the appointed hour was another of those social niceties Californians seemed to regard as being reserved for the mildly eccentric.

We parked in the ground-level garage of the luxury condo, Evie having given me the push-button code to the gate when I called to RSVP. "Don't breathe a word, darling," she'd said. "I don't want the wrong sort crashing the party." I was baffled as to what wrong sort she thought I might reveal this information.

Evie's upper-crust English accent rang out as soon as we got out of the lift and stepped into the lobby of her splendid two-storey digs. "There you are, sweeties," she said, planting a kiss in the air above my left ear, at the same time handing Chamois, her Maltese terrier, to Tony. "And the doggies, too." She looked doubtfully at Watson and Trixie, standing obediently at our sides. "I hope they won't teach Chamois any bad habits while they're here. They'd better stay in Howard's dressing room for the duration, if they don't mind. It's very comfortable, and Rosa can serve their dinner in there."

My concern was less for the dogs' comfort than for the contents of Evie's husband's dressing room, given Trixie's destructive proclivities. But Evie had already taken their leashes and was leading them away, Trixie going eagerly, always up for a new lark, Watson casting a slightly bewildered look at me over her shoulder.

"It's okay," I told her. "Go along with Auntie."

"Howard will be here in just a minute, and he'll show you to your room," Evie said to Tony as she left.

"Don't you bovver about me none, Mrs. C. I can doss down anywhere. We can all muck in together, like," replied Tony, whose expectations of the Cavendishes' hospitality had apparently been more along the lines of sleeping on the couch or, heaven forbid, sharing beds.

I changed in Evie's bedroom. "Are you putting on weight?" she asked, eyeing me critically.

I might well have asked her the same thing. Her caftan, though gorgeous—cream brocade, embroidered with rich threads of gold and silver—hung tentlike from her shoulders, designed to cover a multitude of sins.

"And I don't know about that frock," she continued as I slipped the offending garment over my head. "You must have been either very drunk or very optimistic when you bought that."

Clearly our friendship was not based upon superficial flattery and artifice, but upon a history of shared experiences and mutual affection, demonstrated on my part by overlooking her tendency to be critical of my every move, more overtly on Evie's by her desire for only the best for me, as she proved with her next words.

"Here, try this." She went to the dresser and, taking a diamond necklace from her jewelry case, draped it casually around my throat to see the effect.

"Oh, no. I couldn't," I protested. "It's much too costly. I'd feel uncomfortable."

"Nonsense. I want you to make a good impression. Anyway, it's only paste."

I doubted that. Evie never settled for less than the best. But my experience with real gems being somewhat limited, I had to take her word for it.

While she fastened the glittering pendant around my neck, I apologized on Tony's behalf that he would not be wearing a suit.

"Heavens, not to worry! That's why I put 'dress optional' on the invitation. The dear boy will do very well as he is. I've been thinking of giving him a pair of gold cuff links for his birthday."

This left me completely nonplussed. I had no idea that she knew when Tony's birthday was. It was certainly not information to which I was privy.

"But he doesn't own a dress shirt," I answered weakly.

"We must encourage him to get one, then," she replied with an air of finality that brooked no further discussion, if, indeed, I had been able to come up with a suitable response. To insist that Tony neither wanted nor needed a dress shirt, never mind gold cuff links, would entail pointless argument, as well as appearing a trifle mean-spirited.

"Now promise me you'll make an effort to please," said my friend, putting finishing touches to her already perfectly coiffed ash-blond hair. "I have gone to a great deal of trouble to arrange for some Really Nice Men to be here especially for your benefit."

The suggestion that some kind of extraordinary effort was required to get a man interested in me was not received with unbridled enthusiasm on my part.

Heedless of my groan of annoyance, she continued, "I want none of your quiet-little-mouse act this evening."

"I'm sorry I can't be more like you, tossing *bons mots* around the room like rose petals," I said petulantly. "It's just not in me."

"Now, you've heard of Senator Farley Wellstock, of course," Evie continued, ignoring my protest. "He's been on all the chat shows recently, talking about the drug-smuggling problem. He's an old friend of Howard's from Texas. He's here visiting the Border Patrol stations doing research for his committee."

Actually, I hadn't heard of the senator, but feeling I should make more of an effort to please my friend, I nodded noncommittally as she continued.

"He'd be a wonderful catch. He's only recently come on the market. He really needs cheering up, poor dear. Just getting over a messy divorce, you know." She put her finger to her mouth. "Best not talked about, though," she said, immediately contradicting herself by proceeding to tell all. "He and his ex had a bitter custody battle."

By this time we were making our way downstairs to join the rest of the company already gathered for aperitifs.

I feigned interest. "Really? They have children?"

"Oh, neither of them wants the children. They both want the dogs."

We entered a large dining room where the other guests stood by the window admiring the magnificent sunset over Mission Bay. To my dismay I saw that Evie and I were the only females present.

Talk about dropping me in at the deep end! Apart from Tony and Howard, the only one I recognized was Ted Willoughby, Howard's accountant. Tennis Ted, as

I recalled him after a rather embarrassing encounter we'd had during the Purloined Pooch Affair, in which I had been unfortunately involved a year or so earlier.

Howard came over and greeted me with a warm hug, pressing a tall Pimm's No. 1 into my hand. I drank it thirstily, realizing I'd had nothing to eat or drink all day.

"Bought a caseload the last time we came through the duty-free shop at Heathrow," he said as I expressed surprise. I hadn't had a Pimm's, the recipe for which has been kept secret since its creation in the nineteenth century, since my last trip to England.

Howard introduced me to Max Oberon, his solicitor, a tall, rather distinguished-looking man, impeccably dressed. However, his film-star good looks were no compensation for his conversation, limited as it was to his golf score and his prowess on the tennis court. I considered him vain and self-absorbed, an opinion soon confirmed as he repeatedly admired himself in the mirror over the bar, smoothing back his silver-fox hair with long well-manicured fingers.

Tony, meanwhile, was engaged in conversation with a rather heavyset man I took to be Senator Wellstock. My worst fears were realized as Tony turned toward me and I saw that he was wearing one of those T-shirts with a fake tuxedo painted on the front. Evie, however, had affected not to notice, if indeed she cared, and to judge from the senator's chuckles of appreciation, probably at one of Tony's Cockney anecdotes, his attire bothered no one but myself.

Pimm's and nibbles (excellent shrimp canapes) were followed by a delectable meal prepared by Rosa, Evie's housekeeper. Though originally from Mexico, Rosa had, under Evie's expert tutelage, mastered the mysteries of English cuisine, though occasionally she was unable to resist introducing her salsa and chilis into the blander recipes beloved by her employer.

But today Rosa had held her spicy impulses in check; the menu was English traditional, and contained all my favourites, of which Evie was well aware. A creamy vichyssoise, accompanied by a superb Sauterne, was followed by a tender beef Wellington, tiny roast potatoes, and fresh brussels sprouts, washed down with a French Burgundy.

I was seated between the senator on my right, and Chamois, in his own booster chair, on my left. Knowing Evie's fondness for the little dog, I wasn't surprised that he was allowed to join the company, though I personally agree with author Fran Lebowitz that a dog should not be allowed at the dining table unless he can hold his own in the conversation.

While he was unable to do that, Chamois was responsible for the direction of much of the table talk, Senator Wellstock confiding to me that he had two dogs of his own. "Shorthair pointers," he said proudly. "Best stock from Germany."

"Have a Jack Russell meself," said Tony, helping himself to the horseradish.

"Ever use him for hunting?" asked Wellstock. "Friend of mine out by Ramona breeds them. He's thinking about setting up a hunt for foxes and raccoons and the like."

I set down my Burgundy with trembling hand. The glass tipped and a pool of bloodred wine seeped across the white linen tablecloth. I look upon hunting as cruelty to animals, but with undoubted moral cowardice, I refrained from saying so, remarking only that "I think your friend will find that to be illegal in California, Senator."

I sensed rather than saw the flicker of annoyance on

Evie's face, the look of amusement on Howard's.

"Nonsense," the senator replied. "The fox enjoys it as much as the dogs. Likes the challenge."

I'd never heard such claptrap, but fortunately words failed me, at least those of the rose-petal sort Evie would wish of me. I mopped at the wine with my serviette, and silently cursed Tony for dragging me into this.

Across the table Ted Willoughby gave me a sympathetic smile and changed the subject. "Tell us more about your committee, Senator," he said.

Wellstock needed no encouragement, and for the next ten minutes held forth on his mission to study the problems of the world's busiest land border crossing.

I relieved my boredom by cutting up Chamois's beef Wellington for him. Evie leaned toward me across the table as I was about to pop a morsel into the little dog's mouth.

"Don't give him too much pastry, Dee," she advised, keeping her voice low so as not to interrupt the senator. "It's not good for his little waistline."

I thought of Watson and Trixie banished to Howard's dressing room. No beef Wellington for them, thank goodness. We didn't need any upset tummies on the drive home tomorrow. They would be dining on the dry kibble I'd brought along.

Evie's voice broke into my thoughts. "Isn't that fascinating, Dee?" My face must have shown my bafflement. "The senator's plans for the border?" she prompted. Her tone left no doubt that she was getting impatient with me.

I took a sip from my wineglass, which Rosa had refilled, and tried to take an intelligent interest as Wellstock continued, "It's a tricky job, keeping the traffic flowing freely for the sake of trade and tourism, without sacrificing law enforcement."

For Evie's sake I made an effort. Setting down my wineglass ever so carefully, I turned to the senator and asked, "Do you know anything about exotic-bird smuggling?"

He put down his fork, looking pleased at my interest. "Exotics? No, can't say that I do. Not my field. We leave that kind of environmental crap to the tree huggers." He looked around the table to see if the others enjoyed his joke, then remounted his hobbyhorse. "My area's trade. We're getting complaints from our manufacturers with factories down there. Trouble is, the long waits required by customs and the INS get everybody flustered. Everyone starts to look suspicious, and you can't tell the drug smugglers from the honest citizens. That leads to even longer delays."

It all sounded quite chaotic, and I was not looking forward to our trip across the border the following day. Whether or not Tony sensed my growing apprehension, I don't know, but I was relieved that when the conversation turned to lawbreaking and drug-smuggling, he interrupted Wellstock's expounding with, "Lovely grub, Mrs. C. What's for afters?"

Evie looked pleased. "Your favourite, dear boy. I recall you saying how you missed English apple tart made with Cox's orange pippins. It so happens that the parents sent me a shipment from the farm just last week."

The tart, with a pastry crust made to perfection, just flaky enough not to fall apart on the fork, was served with real Devonshire cream and a dessert wine.

"Tony's certainly the blue-eyed boy around here," I muttered, walking a little unsteadily as Evie and I retired to the drawing room, leaving the men to their cigars and port.

"Dee!" Evie exclaimed in mock disapproval. "I do believe you're a tiny bit tight." She paused while pouring our demitasse coffees from an elegant silver server. "Now, do tell. What do you think of the senator?"

Not for the first time that evening, words failed me.

· 14 ·

El Big!

"WOULDN'T IT MAKE more sense to take the bus?" I asked, observing people queued up at a stop near a large car park.

"Nah," Tony snorted. "That's for tourists. S'long as you know your way around, know where to park, it's more convenient to take your car over."

I trusted his words didn't fit the category of "famous last," but I was in no mood to argue. My head ached and I felt slightly hungover after all the wine of the previous evening. Nobody had been in a hurry to get up that morning. In fact, Evie still hadn't come downstairs when we left, even though by then it was past noon.

Watson and Trixie were to spend the day playing with their friends Chamois and Britt, Howard's Brittany spaniel, a most nonsporting sporting dog. We had left a note asking Evie to have the dogs ready to leave on our return, as we wanted to get back to Surf City that evening. We would use the garage intercom and she or Howard could bring them down to us.

The weather was still cool after the winter storms—in the high sixties. It was good to be wearing comfortable clothes again—my favourite jeans and a lightweight peach-colored twin set, an old British standby which had been in and out of fashion several times. Casual, well-worn mocs on my feet. At least they were more practical than the rubber-thonged sandals Tony insisted on wearing, along with his uniform of black OP shorts and T-shirt. My hair, over which I had taken such pains for the dinner party, had now returned to its customary unruly state—style being an overstatement. In other words, doing exactly what it wanted: decidedly casual, the fringe in dire need of a trim.

Crossing the border was uneventful. Mexican officials quickly waved us through once having satisfied themselves that we carried no firearms, the ban on guns being strictly enforced in Mexico.

To give me a snapshot tour of Tijuana before heading for our appointment, Tony took the long route to the city centre. We drove over roads made spongy by the recent rains, and viewed with dismay the shantytowns among the hilly recesses of the outskirts. Many of the ramshackle homes, built of tarpaper and scrap wood and propped up by stacks of old tires, had been abandoned after the rainstorms had made them uninhabitable.

Things started to look better as we continued through quiet side streets where people sold ceramics and furniture in their front yards, and by the time we reached Avenida Constitución, with its streetside taco stands and vendors hawking brilliantly coloured paper flowers, rustic jewelry, and other crafts, I began to enjoy the restless charm of the city. It was a charm which seemed to reflect the character of its people, who, I had heard, came from all over Mexico to find work in the tourist trade and the rapidly growing assembly factories.

We were to meet Fidel Gomez at the Big Boy restaurant, known locally as "El Big," on Boulevard Agua

Caliente, the city's main drag. My mood took a dive when we parked near the bullring; I was grateful for the fact that no event was scheduled that day and I was spared the *olés* that would have accompanied the taunting of the hapless bulls.

We made our way along the sidewalk past a fish taco stand to the restaurant's entrance.

"Slippery says Fidel is always here in the afternoon, doing business," said Tony.

"Don't tell him I'm a pet detective," I reminded him.

"Not a dickie bird," said Tony, lapsing into Cockney rhyming slang for "not a word."

A friendly, green-uniformed waitress ushered us to a gleaming laminated table. The menu offered a classic transborder mix of fast-food cuisines—coffee, cheeseburgers, enchiladas, and tacos.

Tony ordered two coffees, and asked the waitress if Fidel Gomez was around. The smile left her face as she said. "He is not here yet. He had to go to *el norte* on business, a death in the family." She spoke perfect English, as almost everyone in this border town appeared to do.

While we waited for our coffee I took a good look around. El Big appeared to be a modern-day cantina. Although, according to Tony, who seemed to know more than was good for him about life's seamier side, the talk there often revolved around the sinister, the atmosphere that afternoon appeared disarmingly homey. At the booth next to ours sat a couple with a brood of boisterous small children, while over by the window were a group of solid-looking businessmen who, plunking down their briefcases, had converted their table into an informal office.

I sensed, rather than saw, Fidel's arrival—a commotion at the entrance, a hush in the conversation. I turned to see the waitress nodding in our direction.

Clad in black leather jacket, a cellular phone tucked into a breast pocket, the mustachioed Fidel Gomez joined us, choosing a seat with his back to the wall, where he could keep his eye on the door.

Things went badly from the start.

Addressing Tony, his first words were, "You didn't see me, you didn't talk to me, and you don't know me." A thin cigar smoldered between his fingers. "Now tell me what you want."

Elbows on the table, Tony leaned toward Gomez. "It's like this 'ere, chum. Me mate, Sam Vyper, said you might be able to 'elp us, that is, 'elp Mrs. Doolittle, 'ere."

Turning to me, possibly thinking I was a fellow hobbyist of Slippery Sam's, Fidel said, "Got plenty of baby snakes. Make you good price. Easy to get across the border. Put them in your bra."

" 'Ere, you watch yer language, mate," said Tony, bristling.

Fidel's face grew dark.

"No, not reptiles," I said hastily. "I don't want to buy anything." Then, as Fidel started to get to his feet, as if we were wasting his time: "I'm after information. We're willing to pay." I hoped that whatever the price, it didn't exceed what I had in my purse.

Fidel sat down again. "What kind of information?"

"I'm looking for a lost parrot."

He looked amused. "We send parrots north, we don't bring them south," he said.

"Yes, but we thought you might know someone who deals in exotics who"—I tried to choose my words carefully—"might also know something about stolen birds.

I'm sure you're aware there's money in kidnapping exotics."

"Oh, yes. I'm *aware,*" he said, a slow grin exposing nicotine-stained teeth. "Where are you from?"

I had the sense he was mocking my accent. It happens sometimes that I'll be talking to someone in all seriousness, and suddenly realize that they are listening not so much to what I am saying, but to how I am saying it. It's very off-putting, I can to tell you.

"England," I said, with a polite smile.

"England," he repeated. "You want a green card?"

It occurred to me that smuggling exotics wasn't the only illegal enterprise in which Fidel was involved. "No thank you," I said. "I already have one. Now, to get back to the lost parrot. Would you know anybody who might be able to help us? No questions asked, of course, and we'd be willing to pay a reward. A breeder in Surf City, Vance DeVayne, tells me there's a lot of—"

"DeVayne?" The black look returned to Fidel's face. "He's your amigo?"

I tried to take my cue from Tony, but just at that moment my ally was ogling the waitress.

"You know him?" I asked.

"He killed my nephew, José," Fidel thundered, now on his feet. "My family demands vengeance."

Tony, his attention drawn back to the table by Fidel's menacing tone, but perhaps not getting the serious drift of the conversation, only hearing the melodramatic mention of vengeance, raised his coffee mug in Fidel's direction. "Best of British luck, mate," he said sarcastically. A remark which did not translate well from Brit-speak to Anglo-Spanish.

Fidel snapped open his cell phone and spoke rapidly to someone in Spanish, finishing with *"Ándale, ándale."*

I kicked Tony under the table. I didn't have to be fluent in Spanish to guess that Fidel was summoning reinforcements, and it didn't sound like it was to join us for coffee.

I picked up my purse, ready to leave, giving Fidel a strained smile. "I'm sorry to have taken up your time. I guess you can't help us."

Tony, at last alert to the seriousness of the situation, stood at the same time. "Come on, luv, let's go."

I fumbled in my purse for a ten-dollar bill to pay for our coffee, but Tony pulled me past the cash register and through the door. I looked back to see Fidel get to his feet, a determined look on his face, and head after us.

"Come on, luv. 'Urry up," Tony said again as he hustled me along the sidewalk to the car.

Not looking where he was going, Tony caught one of his ridiculous thongs in a crack in the uneven sidewalk, tripped, and fell into the taco stand, sending the unfortunate vendor and his wares into the gutter.

My heart pounding, I ran past the sprawling vendor, tossing the crumped ten at him as I went. Still lying in the street, he smoothed the bill and put it in his pocket, buying us a little more time, as Fidel slowed to step around him.

Tony had picked himself up and raced after me to the car. But he had trouble starting the engine. Just as I thought he'd flooded it, the starter took hold, and we headed for the border. Looking back, I caught sight of Fidel and the taco vendor getting into a green Chevy low-rider and start to follow.

We couldn't have chosen a worse time. The crossing was a fume-bathed, bumper-to-bumper bottleneck. Senator Wellstock's words came back to me as we joined the international conga line waiting to enter the States. "Chaos," he had called it. Piñata-toting shoppers returning from a day's bargain hunting; commuters from the factories; racetrack aficionados; and tourists from Baja California vacation spots—Ensenada, Rosarita Beach, and points south. Who knew what human and animal cargo might be smuggled here, camouflaged by the sea of cars, vendors, and impatient motorists?

Weaving around the cars waiting to pass through one of the several exit lanes staffed by U.S. Customs inspectors, vendors made the most of their opportunity to hawk their wares one last time. I rolled down my window in an effort to grab some fresh air, the woody not being equipped with air-conditioning, and immediately a young girl thrust in a garishly painted ceramic of a grinning donkey in a straw hat, bearing fruit-laden panniers. With a curt "No, thank you," I hastily closed the window, immediately regretting my abruptness. She wasn't to know that costumed beasts of burden were not my favourite motif.

Nerves frayed, we were getting closer to the barrier when we were delayed by an altercation three cars ahead. A rather large, middle-aged couple in brightly coloured Hawaiian shirts, plus fours, argyle socks, and Nikes, and topped by silver-studded sombreros—a veritable United Nations of attire—was made to unlock their car trunk and unload their purchases, including several that had been elaborately gift-wrapped. The woman wailed while her packages were unceremoniously dumped on the ground and torn open, her partner nervously mopping his brow with a large white handkerchief. I thought I heard a British accent in his protest that they had "nowt to hide."

While we waited I caught sight of the green Chevy

two lanes over. It was several cars behind us, but the line it was in was moving faster. Fidel was gaining on us. It was hopeless to think that he might not spot us in that sea of cars; Tony's surfboard-topped woody was hard to miss.

The sombrero pair were finally waved through, apparently having proven their innocence, as were the next two cars. It was our turn.

" 'Ere goes," said Tony as we drove into the inspection area. "Got yer green card ready?"

"Please be quiet," I murmured. To my mind, Tony, disheveled, with blood congealing on his forehead as a result of his fall, looked far more suspicious than the sombrero pair, however weirdly they were dressed.

But though the inspector studied Tony's face closely, he was apparently satisfied that we carried no contraband and, with a cursory glance at our green cards, nodded for us to be on our way.

By that time there were only five cars between us and the Chevy.

I thought we'd lost them in the freeway traffic, but then, back in San Diego, we had just turned the corner to go up the hill to Evie's condo, when they appeared again. It was almost as if they had known where we were headed and taken a shortcut.

Hastily punching in the code to open the parking garage gate, we drove in, the steel grille clanging shut behind us. We were safe. But Fidel turned off the engine and parked across the street, apparently prepared to wait us out.

I called Evie on the garage intercom, and she soon joined us, with Watson and Trixie in tow.

I explained the situation. "Should we call the police?" I asked.

Evie's reaction was not unexpected. "Really, Dee," she said, peering at the Chevy and its passengers, "you are the absolute limit! Not only do you get yourself into more trouble than obviously either one of you is capable of handling, but you then have the bloody nerve to lead said trouble right to my doorstep." She paused for breath. "But no, we won't call the police. I don't want the neighbours disturbed."

Before we could stop her, she was out of the garage by a side door, and approaching the Chevy with the determined air of one who did not suffer fools gladly.

Her cut-glass tones carried clearly across the street. "What in God's name do you think you're doing, lurking about here? This is a private community."

Fidel must have said something about looking for an address.

"There's no one here by that name. So clear off. You're trespassing."

Whether it was Evie's words or the fortuitous appearance at that very moment of a private security patrol car coming over the hill, the Chevy took off, as fast as the posted speed allowed.

We bundled Watson and Trixie into the car and made our way back down the hill, having quite forgotten to say our adieus to Evie, never mind our thank-yous.

I knew I would never hear the last of that.

· 15 ·

Checkpoint

"SHE'S A CAUTION, that Mrs. C," said Tony as we entered the I-5 freeway ramp.

I agreed absentmindedly that Evie was indeed a character. My attention was focused on the road behind us, watching for our pursuers, but I could see no sign of the green Chevy.

I reached over to pet Watson and Trixie, who, sensing they were homeward bound, had settled down to sleep on the backseat.

"It's all been for nothing," I complained, facing forward again. "We've wasted the entire day on a wild-goose chase, upset Evie, and have absolutely nothing to show for our pains. I'm still no further forward in finding Scarlett O'Hara."

"Who?"

"Mrs. Handley's macaw."

"Oh. Well, I don't know as 'ow you can say *nothing*," said Tony. "I think we got something useful out of ol' Gomez."

"What's that?" I could think of no benefit that had come from our encounter with our TJ connection.

"We know that José is Gomez's nephew, for one thing."

"So?"

"Gomez deals in smuggled birds; José's accused of stealing birds. Then José turns up dead, and you say the police found fevvers in his truck."

I nodded. "José and his uncle were working together, for sure. What else?"

"Gomez thinks that chap DeVayne had something to do with José's murder."

"And that's absurd," I said. "Vance readily admitted to Detective Mallory that he'd had a dustup with José over the stolen fledglings. He made no attempt to hide it."

"Not much point, was there, when the police already knew about it."

I had to concede that, but I was reluctant to think that the nice young man and his sweet sister were anything other than what they appeared to be: a bit over-the-top when it came to birds, but otherwise a charming couple without a malicious bone between them.

I said as much to Tony. "I know you haven't met him, but you can take my word for it. He's no murderer. Gomez is angry and lashing out at the most obvious suspect. He probably knows all about the row over the fledglings. There's something else going on that we haven't fathomed yet. Someone else has to be involved."

I looked behind me again for signs of the green Chevy. But it was getting dark; I would not be able to spot our pursuers, if indeed they were still tailing us.

Tony read my thoughts. "Don't worry, luv. They won't have bothered to come this far; not unless they had other reasons for coming, anyway."

He was probably right. But the thought that Gomez might have other quarry in mind, quite apart from ourselves, made me say, "I tell you what, though. As soon as I get home, I'm going to call Vance and warn him about Gomez's threats."

Tony slowed as we approached the Border Patrol's San Clemente checkpoint. About seventy miles north of the Mexican border, the station was intended as a last-ditch effort to catch smugglers and illegal aliens before they escaped to the anonymity of Los Angeles.

There were several cars ahead of us in our lane, but it was an orderly procedure, nothing like the chaotic scene at the border. Most cars were being waved through, barely stopping. But, as luck would have it, a Dodge van several cars ahead was stopped for inspection, causing a delay in all lanes.

"Not again," I groaned.

I got out of the car to stretch my legs. A man who had been in the car immediately behind the van had also got out, and was walking back along the line. He stopped to light a cigarette, and as he took the first puff, he looked up and gave me a friendly nod.

"Is it drugs?" I asked.

"No," he said, blowing smoke through his nostrils. "Something to do with birds. He had them hidden inside the spare tire; their legs and beaks were bound with tape."

"How awful," I said. But before I could question him further, the van was driven to one side, the traffic started to move again, and I got back into the car. The driver of the van was being led away in handcuffs. As he passed under the bright lights of the Border Patrol building, I thought I recognized him.

"Wasn't that Little Bob?" I said to Tony as we were waved through the checkpoint.

"Little Bob? Where?" said Tony, looking in the wrong direction.

"Too late," I said, then realizing something that I hadn't had a chance to sort out in my thoughts during the day's craziness: "That's who it is!"

"That's who what is?"

"The missing link! It's Little Bob! Right from the start you said that the body we found on the beach looked like his friend Joe." I gave his shoulder a gentle push. "Don't you get it? Joe turns out to be José, José stole the macaw, worked for Vance, and is Gomez's nephew. And now here's Little Bob, caught red-handed smuggling birds." I clapped my hands in triumph. "We're getting warmer, old boy."

Trixie and Watson stirred on the backseat, hoping that the commotion meant they were home. Seeing that they weren't, they settled down to sleep again.

"You reckon?" Tony considered my theory for a minute or two, then continued, "And then there's 'is mum, up to 'er behind in parrots."

I thought back to those last few minutes at the Big Boy. Had Gomez, thinking we were onto him, been telling his operatives to move Little Bob and the birds quickly, with his cell-phone *"ándales"*?

WATSON RAN AHEAD of me up the driveway, as happy as I was to be home. As I approached the front door I heard whistling coming from inside the house. Watson heard it, too, and stood stock-still, listening, ears pricked in alertness.

The strains of "Hello, Dolly" wafted through the keyhole. Of all the cheek! Not only had the burglar entered my home uninvited, but he was nonchalantly whistling while he helped himself to my valuables. Though, in truth, I owned so little of real value that I'd have had to help him find something worth stealing.

Holding my keys in a firm grip to keep them from jangling, I quietly unlocked the door, pushed it open, and let Watson go in first, to flush out the intruder. She hesitated, uncertain, in the small entryway, then sat, with her head cocked to one side, staring into the sitting room as if trying to figure something out. She certainly didn't look as if there was anything to be afraid of. I took a step closer and followed her stare. I drew my breath in surprise.

It was the cockatiel. Twenty-four hours' peace and quiet had allowed it to recover from its trauma, and it was now feeling well enough to run through its repertoire. I had left the sitting-room light on to make the house looked occupied in my absence, as was my practice, quite forgetting that the bird might not be able to settle down for the night.

"Well," I said to Watson. "Boy or girl, its name is Dolly from now on."

I fed Watson, checked on Hobo's food and water, made myself a cup of tea, then with notebook and pen in hand settled down to play back the two messages blinking on the answer machine.

But before I could press the playback button the phone rang. A faint, crackly voice I barely recognized as Vance DeVayne's came over the wire.

"Delilah. Help me. I'm dying."

· 16 ·

Sweet Tweets Revisited

I WAS HALFWAY to Sweet Tweets before I realized I should have called the police first.

Why had Vance called me, anyway? We hardly knew each other. Surely it would have been easier to dial 911? It wasn't until much later that I learned the answer to that question.

There were plenty of other questions to occupy my mind on my way through the quiet Surf City streets on a late evening.

"Fidel Gomez must have made good on his threat already, but I don't see how he had the time, even if he passed us on the freeway," I said to Watson, who, sitting alongside me, was none too thrilled to be on the road again so soon after arriving home. At this time on a typical day she'd have been dozing alongside me on the couch while I read or watched television.

I found Vance in the store, lying on the tiled floor in a pool of his own blood. He wasn't dead, but he might well have been forgiven for thinking he was on his way out. He had been badly beaten around the head, but I could see no sign of a weapon. The room was otherwise undisturbed, indicating he'd had no opportunity to defend himself. He must have been taken by surprise.

I called 911 straightaway.

There was no sign of Vera. If this was Fidel's work, might he have kidnapped her? I remembered how flustered she had appeared when José's name was mentioned on my first visit to Sweet Tweets. Was she somehow involved in the smuggling business, and perhaps not quite as innocent as she seemed? Surely not.

Afraid I might find her lying injured like Vance, or worse, I began to look around, holding Watson close to my side.

From outside came the sound of a gate banging. I went to the back door and called, "Vera, are you there?"

There was no reply. Apart from the sound of the gate, it was eerily quiet. The birds had all gone to roost, silent now, except for an occasional twitter when one or another of them shifted its position, disturbing its mate.

I flipped on the switch by the door and the outside area flooded with light. Birds squawked in surprise at the sudden dawn. The gate of the first aviary swung idly in the light breeze. I moved to close it, hoping that the Hyacinth macaws hadn't already escaped. But I was too late. They were gone. As I pulled the gate handle toward me I felt a sticky substance on my hand. It was blood. Had it come from one of the macaws, or was it the thief's?

I tried calling for Vera again. If she answered, I never heard.

I did hear Watson's warning growl, and in the clear night air was conscious also of the faint smell of a cheap aftershave lotion or cologne. Suddenly I was shoved from behind, and fell forward into the empty cage, striking my head on the concrete. I heard Watson yelp, and the gate slam shut behind me. Then the noise of a vehicle revving up, followed soon afterward by the welcome sound of approaching police sirens.

"GET AWAY! DAMN dog!" Offley was saying gruffly.

From my prone position I could see his black-booted foot kicking out at Watson.

Watson, a sheep in wolf's clothing if ever there was one, would be puzzled by such treatment.

Offley reached for his pistol and I was raising my head to protest when another pair of shoes arrived, dark brown Rockports.

"She's harmless," said Detective Mallory. "Just catch hold of her and tie her up somewhere."

For one shocking moment, I thought he was talking about me.

He turned and looked down at me through the metal gate. "Deli—er, Mrs. Doolittle. I hope there's an explanation for you being here."

His words were harsh, but beneath the exasperation I believed I detected a note of concern.

He opened the gate and helped me to my feet.

"Who did this? Are you all right? Come and sit down."

We English don't care to make a fuss, especially when it's entirely possible our problems might well be laid at our own door. I ought to have called the police sooner, as I was sure Mallory was about to point outto me.

But he kept his own counsel as I replied offhandedly, "I'll be all right in a minute. Just had the stuffing knocked out of me a bit, that's all. And no, I have no idea who did it."

He took my arm and led the way back into the store, where the paramedics were tending to Vance, and the evidence technicians were already going about their appointed tasks of securing the scene—taking photographs, dusting for fingerprints, measuring distances—with all the efficiency I had come to expect of anyone associated with Detective Mallory.

He told Offley to see if he could determine if anything had been stolen.

"The Hyacinths are gone," I said. "I don't know about anything else."

"Flowers, Mrs. Doolittle?" Impatiently Mallory ran his fingers through his hair. "This is no time to be worrying about flowers. We have a serious case of assault here. Murder, if DeVayne doesn't survive."

"No. You don't understand. Hyacinth *macaws*. The most valuable birds in the place."

Offley cleared his throat. "That's the fifth reported parrot theft from area pet shops this year," he said.

I was beginning to understand why Mallory tolerated the gruff sergeant. He was capable of the kind of stolid, persistent attention to tedious detail for which the senior detective was perhaps not temperamentally suited.

Catching sight of the blood on my hand, Mallory said, "You're hurt. Let's take a look."

"No. It's not mine. It came from the cage gate outside. Somebody's been hurt." I moved over to a drinking-water fountain by the door, and attempted to wipe my hand clean with a tissue.

"You're lucky it wasn't you," he said, sounding relieved. "The fact that you're here means you know more than is good for you about this business. Do you have any idea who could have done this?"

I shook my head. "There are only two people I know of who might have a motive, and they both have alibis."

His interest quickened. "I'll be the judge of that," he said.

I hesitated, reluctant to tell him about my disastrous trip with Tony to Tijuana, the meeting with Gomez, and the consequent chase down the freeway.

"I don't want to talk about it," I said.

"Well, I do. I'm one of those people who, when someone doesn't want to talk about something, that's exactly what I do want to talk about," he said sternly.

We stood aside while the paramedics placed poor Vance onto a gurney and trundled him out to the waiting ambulance. Looking at his pale, still face, I was overcome with a need to help in whatever way I could.

"The most important thing is to get those birds back," I said urgently. "Vance has a small fortune tied up in them. Why don't you put out one of your APBs or missing-persons reports, or whatever it is you do on these occasions?"

"We don't put out APBs on birds," Mallory said grimly. "We leave that to you pet detectives."

But for once I refused to rise to the bait. It had been a long day and I was quite done in by it all.

He seemed to sense my exhaustion. Looking around at the scene as if to satisfy himself that all were doing their jobs to his satisfaction, he said, "Maybe you'd like to go for a cup of coffee somewhere and talk?"

I hadn't eaten all day, what with my hangover in the morning, and our adventures on the road since. "Thank you. I really am feeling rather faint. Perhaps a cup of tea . . ." A thought occurred to me. "You know, there's a restaurant quite near here where they have a Hyacinth macaw on display. You could see exactly what it is that's been stolen."

I locked Watson in the empty Hyacinth cage, telling Offley that she was not to be let out under any circumstances short of fire or earthquake. And having assured myself that she would be safe in my absence, I readily accepted Mallory's invitation, welcoming the opportunity to show him once and for all that I was not the interfering busybody he took me for.

Mallory gave instructions to Offley to secure the area, to keep searching for the weapon, and to call him the minute Vera showed up. Then, for the second time that evening, he took my arm—a habit I decided I could very easily get used to—and ushered me out to his car.

. 17 .

Rainforest Rendezvous

"WELCOME TO THE Rainforest Restaurant."

The two live macaws on adjoining T-stands chorused the greeting as they swayed from one foot to the other, swinging their heads forward as if trying to get a better look at us. One was a stunning blue and gold, the other the promised Hyacinth. I pointed it out to Mallory, saying again, "They're probably the most valuable of all the exotic birds."

But other than making good on my offer to show him an example of just what it was that the thief at Sweet Tweets had probably made off with, I wasn't sure that my suggestion had been such a good idea after all.

The restaurant had been designed for the young in search of distraction. We were neither. All we wanted was a quiet place to sit and talk.

Instead, on entering the bright, noisy eatery, we found ourselves immersed in an interactive dining experience amidst a menagerie of robotic animals in a rainforest setting of larger-than-life banyan trees and waterfalls. The sounds of carefully orchestrated tropical thunderstorms, jungle drums, and assorted bellows and roars conspired to reduce conversation to a minimum, and had obviously been designed for the benefit of people who had very little to say to each other.

While we waited to be seated, I asked the young safari-garbed host if he knew who took care of the macaws.

"Our birds are very well looked after. They come out to visit for no more than two hours at a time," he assured me, sounding somewhat like a robotic parrot himself. "They're all second and third generation, domestically bred, and hand-raised. None of them comes from the rain forest," he hastened to add. From his defensive tone I guessed he got that question a lot.

Mallory was apparently as amused as I was by the young man's earnest protestations. "What did you expect?" he asked, taking my arm yet again as, intent on dodging a snake dangling from a tree branch, I almost stumbled into the gaping jaws of a yawning hippo. "Confessions of illegal imports?"

The host led us past whimsical butterflies, frogs and crocodiles, trumpeting elephants and cascading waterfalls, to a table where we were seated under the curious gaze of a mechanical gorilla.

The fear that my choice of restaurant had been a mistake was confirmed when, upon reviewing the menu, I belatedly realized that this was not the place to find a decent cup of tea. I settled for coffee and, desperate for sustenance, selected, not without some misgivings, the Jungle Rumble, a concoction of turkey, salsa, tomatoes, and fried onions stuffed into pita bread.

Annoyingly, Mallory only ordered coffee, and watched while I ate.

Adding to my uneasiness was the awareness that I was still in my jeans and twin set, decidedly grubby after the day's adventures, and now I was shocked to notice in the bright light, stained with something I was rather afraid was Vance's blood. Hardly the outfit I would have chosen for a *tête-à-tête* with Mallory. I wished I'd had the foresight and the time to change into my tan linen trouser suit, the most reliable all-purpose outfit I owned. Ideal for a first date. Not that this qualified as a date, I told myself sternly.

Mallory, on the other hand, always looked well turned out, tonight wearing a light brown suit, brown shirt, and beige tie. There was a slightly sporty quality to his wardrobe, a little more dash than one might have expected of a policeman. Maybe his seniority allowed him a certain latitude, I thought. He must be nearing retirement, and I wondered idly about his future plans. I understood he was unmarried, though whether divorced or widowed I had yet to discover. Since we had left Sweet Tweets, he had made no attempt to call home to let anyone know he would be late, so as far as I could tell, there was no significant other waiting anxiously by the telephone.

After we placed our order, I went to the ladies' room hoping to make myself look more presentable. But the tired face and untidy hair reflected in the ill-lit mirror was enough to discourage anybody's romantic thoughts. I couldn't blame it all on the poor lighting, I decided.

But if he was aware of the mess I looked, Mallory was kind enough to act as if he didn't notice.

As soon as the food was served, he got straight to the point. "So tell me . . ." He paused while a talking banyan tree boomed out an environmental message. "What were you doing at Sweet Tweets?"

"I arrived home from San Diego around nine this evening. About half an hour later Vance called me for help."

"Why call you? Why not simply dial 911?"

"I've asked myself the same thing," I said between

mouthfuls of turkey and onions. "Maybe it had something to do with my case."

Mallory raised bushy eyebrows in question.

"A lost pet macaw. Vance knew about it. I told you the other day."

He nodded. "You also said something about two people with alibis. You're very well informed for someone whose only goal is to find a lost parrot."

"Macaw," I corrected. "There's a difference. Did you notice the birds at the entrance? Macaws have the long tails—"

"Don't change the subject," he interrupted impatiently. "Get back to the two suspects you claim to know about."

He certainly knew how to press my buttons.

"Claim, indeed. I know for a fact."

He smiled. He had achieved his purpose. There was nothing for it. I had to tell him. He listened with interest, occasionally allowing a grin to cross his face as I related how Tony and I had met Fidel Gomez at El Big in Tijuana.

But his expression turned to one of concern as I told him, between pauses necessitated first by a mock thunderclap that rumbled overhead, then later by a bull elephant roaring its way out of the fake forest, of how the meeting had turned ugly, and of the ensuing chase across the border.

He really did seem to care about me.

"When are you going to learn to leave the investigating to the pros?" he demanded. "You might have been hurt. And Tipton's involved in this, too? He should've known better than to take you along. What were you doing down there, anyway?"

"Hoping to find a clue on Scarlett O'Hara."

He smiled at the name. "And who's Scarlett O'Hara?"

I sighed. What was the matter with the man? Wasn't he paying attention? "The lost macaw, of course."

"Right. Go on."

"It turns out that Gomez is the uncle of José Martinez, the man who drowned last week." I took a sip of my coffee. All this talking was making my throat dry. "Anyway, when I mentioned Vance DeVayne, Gomez was furious. He claimed Vance had killed his nephew, and carried on alarming, swearing vengeance."

Mallory leaned forward, one elbow on the table, chin in hand. "Then what happened?"

"We left in a hurry, but like I said, Gomez followed us."

"How do you know he was following you?"

"He showed up at my friend Evie's house in San Diego."

"Mrs. Cavendish?" He obviously had a memory for names. He'd met Evie before, during a previous escapade, but still . . . "So she's mixed up in it, too?"

I shuddered at the possibility of the police questioning Evie about all of this.

"No, she isn't," I said crossly. "She knows nothing about it."

I played with the remains of the pita bread, breaking it into bite-size pieces which I had no intention of eating. I was full. "Anyway, even if Gomez had overtaken us on the freeway, he couldn't possibly have had enough time to reach Sweet Tweets, beat up Vance, and steal the birds before I got back to Surf City. Besides, the burglar was still there when I got there—or somebody was."

Mallory shook his head doubtfully. "You know what I think?"

I was astonished. He was going to confide in me.

"I think DeVayne killed José Martinez and that Martinez's uncle, this Fidel Gomez, went to the bird farm to make good on his threat, and left Vance for dead."

"But I told you, he didn't have time."

"You could be mistaken about the time that elapsed after you got home."

"I don't make those kinds of mistakes," I said sharply. "But why are you so fixed on Vance as José's killer? You said yourself that it's been difficult to pinpoint the exact time of his death. That surely opens up the possibility of multiple suspects. Maybe Gomez killed his nephew, and all that carrying on about vengeance was just a smoke screen."

Not very likely, I had to admit. But I just couldn't accept that Vance was the culprit. In my mind's eye, I saw again his pale face as he lay on the gurney. "You're being too hard on Vance DeVayne," I said.

Mallory leaned back in his chair and loosened his tie in frustration. "Too hard! I'm paid to be hard. Being soft means you get taken advantage of. It certainly sounds as if that's what's happened to you."

"And the missing Hyacinths?"

"Maybe Gomez took them, or maybe DeVayne turned them loose himself, to collect on the insurance." He jotted something in his notebook.

"And who pushed me into the flight cage?"

"It was dark. You could have tripped and fallen, and—"

"Imagined the whole thing, I suppose." I was getting cross. "Thanks a lot. You obviously don't have a very high opinion of me. Not only am I a poor judge of character, but I also can't tell the time, and I don't look where I'm going."

Mercifully, all possible disagreement came to a halt for the next few seconds as our voices were drowned out by another clap of thunder, followed by the hiss of rain and a rather annoying light mist falling around us.

That little rainforest drama over, Mallory picked up the conversation once more.

"What about the second suspect you think has an alibi?"

The man was relentless.

"On our way home from San Diego this evening, at the San Clemente checkpoint, we saw a man taken into custody for bird smuggling—" I paused while the elephant trumpeted an encore. "You see how it keeps coming back to birds? Anyway, I'm pretty sure it was Little Bob Briscoe."

Mallory consulted his notes. I had the feeling this wasn't the first time he'd heard the name.

"Why would you consider Briscoe a suspect?"

Oh dear. I was going to have to mention Tony again. "Because Tony Tipton says that José Martinez was a friend of Little Bob's, who just happens to be Tony's neighbour."

I felt terrible, dragging Tony into this. He couldn't escape his unfortunate reputation. He didn't need the police poking into his background again. After all, he was now, as he had protested to me often enough, "walking the straight and narrer."

But Mallory made no comment regarding my Cockney friend. "What makes you say these, er, Hyacinth macaws are so valuable?" he said.

"Vance told me that his mating pair was worth in the region of thirty thousand dollars."

Mallory raised his eyebrows in surprise. "That's a lot of money for a couple of parrots. Sorry, macaws." He smiled, then continued, "But I guess I can see where they might be an attractive target to some thiefs."

"Oh. Why's that?"

"The penalties for possession of stolen birds are far less than, let's say, for narcotics." He shook his head, then continued, "I don't know, though. Just finding a customer with that kind of cash to spend on birds might take some time."

"The thief knew what he was after, I'm convinced of that," I said. "No one in his right mind would steal them unless he already had a customer. He couldn't advertise, they would be conspicuous if offered on the open market. And they'd be troublesome to care for and keep hidden, what with the noise and everything."

"You keep saying 'he.' Couldn't it just as easily have been a woman?"

I shrugged, not willing right then to voice the thought that was occurring to me even as he spoke, as the memory came flooding back of hitting the hard floor of the Hyacinths' cage, the roaring noise in my ears, the offensive but familiar odour in my nostrils.

Mallory picked up on my distraction. "Is there something you're not telling me?" It was a statement, not a question.

I didn't want to float any more theories only to have them trashed. Yet I supposed I would have to tell him all I knew if I expected him to solve the case and, in doing so, lead me to Scarlett O'Hara.

"Well, back there in the aviary this evening, there was this smell. I've noticed it before, though I can't quite place where or when," I said.

"What kind of a smell was it?"

"Maybe an aftershave or cologne."

"Could it have been an air freshener they use there, or a disinfectant?"

I shook my head. "No, I don't think so. It was more like a cheap perfume."

I'm not sure he heard that last part, and I know I couldn't hear his reply, drowned out as it was by the thundering roar of a stampede on the Serengeti.

This conversation could not go on indefinitely. It was too much of a strain. I think we both breathed a sigh of relief when we could decently bring the meeting to a close. Mallory hailed the server and paid the bill, even though he'd only had coffee. I was too tired to protest that I should have picked up the tab.

I might have hoped for a better outcome. Certainly I wished I could have made a better impression: of a sharp, witty colleague on top of her game, perhaps. Or a glamorous spy with secrets to share—with the right person. As it was, I prayed I would never have to endure such an arduous encounter again.

No, the Rainforest rendezvous had not been a good idea. Not at all.

· 18 ·

Best-Laid Plans

OVERWROUGHT AND SUFFERING from indigestion (the Jungle Rumble had been well named), I spent a restless night dreaming of chaotic border crossings and pursuit by a flying police car driven by Mallory, with the odd sombrero couple as passengers.

I slept rather later than usual and was awakened suddenly by the sound of Watson barking and a loud thumping on the front door. Throwing on my old pink candlewick dressing gown and commanding Watson to stay, I walked stiffly to the front door. My arthritis was playing me up, no doubt a result of my experience in the aviary combined with the rainforest mists of the previous evening.

Was I still dreaming? There on the doorstep stood my nightmare personified in the shape of the couple I had observed at the Mexican border. *Sans* sombreros, but still sporting the Hawaiian shirts and plus fours.

The man spoke first. "We've coom for our Bertie." I'd been right about the British accent. He was from England's North Country.

I stared at them blankly, still trying to make a connection between the couple at the border, my nightmare, and these people at my front door.

I shook my head. "You must be mistaken," I said. "There's no one here by that name."

The man looked at the piece of paper in his hand, then up at the house number.

"Are you Delilah Doolittle, pet detective?"

"Yes but—"

"Then you're the one who called us and said you've got our dog, Bertie." He hesitated. "The Basset? Didn't you get our telephone call?"

The penny finally dropped. "Oh, I'm sorry," I said, remembering the unplayed calls on the answer machine. "I got in too late last night to check my messages."

I shivered in the cool morning air. I could hardly keep them standing on the doorstep while I explained. "Perhaps you'd better come in."

They entered together, their combined girth barely managing to squeeze through the tiny doorway.

The man explained that they had been on tour from their home in Elko, Nevada, to Ensenada, Mexico, when "we stopped at Disneyland, then had dinner at a restaurant."

His wife took up the story. "We let poor Bertie out to do his business. We were looking at the map, trying to decide the best way to get to the San Diego freeway, and we each thought the other had put him back in the car. We didn't miss him until we got to our hotel in San Diego. He's old, you see, and real quiet. Poor little lad. Fair spoiled our holiday, I can tell you."

The man spoke again. "The missus here, she wanted to turn back, right then and there, but as I says to 'er, I've spent hard-earned brass on this 'oliday, and by gum, I'm not going back til I've had me money's worth. So we made up flyers, and the people at the SPCA in San Diego helped us to mail them."

"Money's worth of trouble is all we got," put in the missus. "What with them sods at the border, sorting through our bits and bobs. Wish we'd never left 'ome. And now you're telling us you don't 'ave our Bertie."

"Aye," echoed her husband, looking around as if he expected the Basset to materialize. "Where t' 'ell's our Bertie?"

If they'd only have paused for breath long enough, I would have been able to put their minds at ease.

"He's not here, but he's quite safe at the shelter," I said when I could finally get a word in.

I smoothed my hair and pulled my dressing gown closer around me. "You'll have to excuse me, I've only just got up. Give me a minute and I'll write down the directions for you."

Then, remembering my manners, I said, "I was just about to make tea. Would you like a cup?"

"Wouldn't say no," the man said, settling down on the sitting-room couch and petting Watson, who had gone over to check him out.

Out of habit I reached for my every-day Brown Betty teapot, then immediately realized that it was in pieces in the dustbin, thanks to Dolly bird. Of course, no self-respecting Englishwoman has only one teapot to her name, but my next favourite was larger, and of fine bone china. I would just have to be extra careful and keep it out of Dolly's way until I could get a replacement for Brown Betty from the British Grocer store, my source of all homegrown comforts from sweets, Marmite, and biscuits to electric teakettles and Christmas crackers.

"Lovely cup of tea, m'dear," said the missus a short while later. "I was just saying to 'is nibs 'ere this morning, we 'aven't 'ad a good cuppa since we left 'ome."

Alf and Gert Pickles—as the couple were called—

were a jolly pair and seemed delighted to meet a fellow Brit, and we chatted for a while about our respective hometowns. At any other time I would have enjoyed their company, but having got up late that morning after a very strenuous day, I really was in no mood to entertain. I just wished they would hurry up and leave so I could restart my day. But they seemed to be in no rush once they understood that Bertie was safe and secure.

There seemed to be a very real danger of them settling in for the day. They even suggested that since they hadn't seen the seaside since their last charabanc (what we Brits call a sightseeing motorcoach) outing to Blackpool, they might like to take a walk down to the pier before lunch. At that I decided that the only way to get rid of them was to offer to personally escort them to the shelter, and suggested they follow me in my car. That way I could be sure the Basset was indeed theirs and that there had been no mix-up.

Bertie himself left me in no doubt about that. As soon as he saw his owners walk down the kennel row, it was as if he regained his puppyhood, first bouncing excitedly against the bars of the cage, then running in circles, howling as only a Basset can.

"Ee, there's a good lad, then," said Gert, easing her heavy figure to a crouch so she could pet him while Alf took himself off to the kennel office to pay Bertie's bail. "Now, don't take on so. We'll soon 'ave ee out of there."

Back in the parking lot we said our good-byes as we prepared to go our separate ways.

"Ee by gum, but it's been nice to meet you, Delilah," they duetted. Then, amidst hugs and effusive invitations to be sure to look them up in the unlikely event I ever found myself in Elko, Nevada, Alf and Gert Pickles finally headed for the freeway.

They had offered to pay me the reward, but since all it cost me was the price of a telephone call, I declined, suggesting instead that they make a donation to their local humane society.

On the drive home, my mind free at last to mull over the events of the last few days, it occurred to me, somewhat belatedly, that I'd better ring Tony and warn him to be prepared for a visit from Mallory.

TONY, FULL OF Cockney cheer as always, answered the phone. " 'Allo, Mrs. D. What can I do for you this fine day?"

"Not surfing this morning?" I asked.

"Nah. Waves are too choppy from the storm that's still 'anging about."

"I'm glad I caught you in," I said, going on to relate what had happened at Sweet Tweets the previous evening—the break-in, the attack on Vance, and the theft of the Hyacinth macaws.

"Get away!" Tony kept saying at intervals throughout the story. Then, when I had concluded, "Do you think it was Gomez?"

"No. I'm sure he didn't have time to get there. And even if he did, I think he's too smart to have stolen the Hyacinths, not unless he had a ready customer. I can't think of anyone who would be that stupid."

"I can."

"Can what?"

"Think of someone stupid enough to steal birds without knowing where they were going to unload 'em."

"Who?"

"Bobbi Briscoe. She's always wheeling and dealing

birds." He chuckled at his pun. "Get it, wheeling on 'er 'Arley? And she's none too swift in the brains department, neiver, if you ask me. 'Member we was saying only yesterday that she and Little Bob could be mixed up in this lark?"

I agreed he could be right.

"What does Mallory think?" he then asked.

"He thinks it's Gomez."

"And the missing birds?"

"He says Vance could have turned them loose to claim the insurance money. Though I seem to remember Vance saying the premiums were too dear and he didn't carry any. But Mallory's still of the opinion that Vance killed José." I shook my head. "It's like he's trying to force the puzzle pieces to fit together. He's like a dog with a bone with this theory. He just won't give it up."

I looked at the clock on the kitchen wall. "It's almost noon, Tony. I've got to go. I have calls from yesterday to return, and I'm still no closer to finding Mrs. Handley's macaw."

"Hang on a tick," he said. "I've got an idea."

"Well, if it's anything like your last brilliant brainstorm, I'm not interested," I said, still smarting over our wasted trip to Mexico.

Tony ignored the dig. "I bin 'aving a bit of a think about what you said yesterday about it being Little Bob what was arrested at the checkpoint. If you're right, and then there's 'is mum with all them birds, how about we go over to 'er place later on and do a bit of snooping?"

"And what's she going to think about that?"

"Nah. Not when she's there. We wait till the coast is clear, like, then go and take a shufty. Suss out her trailer. See if we can't get something on 'er. Who knows? Maybe we'll find that Scarlett O'Hara of your'n."

I didn't like the idea at all. But it did serve to remind me of the purpose of my call. "I don't know, Tony. Mallory's already suspicious of you. That's why I called. To warn you I had to tell him that you were with me when I met Gomez in TJ."

"Fan-bloody-tastic," said Tony. "That's all I need. The old Bill on me tail again."

Now he was making me feel bad. I was responsible for the fact that suspicion, however marginal, had been thrown on him when he was trying to help me out. I also knew that finding Scarlett O'Hara and, with any luck, the Hyacinths as well, would be the best way of helping him if it gave us some useful information to pass along to Mallory.

"Come on, luv," Tony was saying. "If she comes home, we'll tell her we just stopped by for a chat. Butter 'er up. I can 'andle 'er."

"I've no doubt you can," I said, reluctantly agreeing and arranging to meet him at his trailer later that evening.

I was about to retrieve my messages when the phone rang again.

"Hallo, Delilah. This is Jack."

I didn't know Detective Mallory and I were on a first-name basis. I was quite certain I had never called him Jack.

"I wondered if you were free for dinner tonight," he went on. "I'll choose the place this time." I could just imagine that sardonic grin of his.

"I can't tonight," I said abruptly. I certainly had no intention of putting myself through that ordeal again. Besides, I had already promised Tony. I could hardly tell Mallory I had an appointment to do a little breaking and entering.

"Some other time, then."

He sounded noncommittal, and I felt compelled to ask, "What was it you wanted to see me about?"

His voice got easier, as if he felt on firmer ground. "DeVayne's still unconscious, and there's no sign of his sister. That makes you the designated expert. We need more information on the stolen birds."

Detective Mallory asking my advice? Was it just an excuse to call? Or was he keeping a copper's eye on me?

"You were right about L. B. Briscoe," he continued. "We've confirmed his alibi with Border Control. But there's still no trace of Gomez. We'll have to take your word on him—for the time being, at least."

"Point of clarification," I said. "Did you just call me an expert?"

"What I meant was, you're the best we've got at the moment."

I didn't try to hide my disappointment. "I knew I must be mistaken," I said stiffly.

He said he would try to reach me sometime the following day, then hung up.

I felt disquieted, without knowing why. I didn't want to go to dinner with him and subject myself to another cross-examination. And I did have a prior engagement. But maybe he really had wanted to make it up to me for last night's disastrous meal.

"And maybe pigs can fly," I said to Watson. "It's just information he's after. And anyway, if he wants company badly enough, I'm sure he has lots of friends he can call." This, followed by the thought that maybe I had been the last on his list, rather than the first, gave me absolutely no comfort at all.

Finally I got around to playing back the neglected

messages. The first, as I expected, was from Bertie the Basset's people. That was all taken care of.

The second, however, was more troublesome.

Beep: "Delilah. It's Evie. Pick up, pick up. Do be a sweetie and pick up. You know I cannot stand these wretched machines. Exciting news. I have to tell you all about the senator. He thinks you are absolutely charming and is quite dying to see you again. We must plan our strategy carefully. You can expect me the day after to-morrow, mid-morning. First things first, we must get you a stunning new wardrobe."

• 19 •

The Caper

"WE'RE ALL SET," said Tony when I arrived at his trailer later that day. "The coast is clear."

He had phoned Bobbi on the pretext of asking her out for a beer, and learned that she was taking off that afternoon to go and get Little Bob out of what she referred to as "some kind of jam" in San Diego and wouldn't be back until the following morning.

Tony had been having a fry-up—eggs, tomatoes, fried bread, bacon, and sausages. It's strange how, of all our senses, that of smell can summon memories the quickest. One whiff from Tony's frying pan and I was transported back to my mother's kitchen on a Sunday morning, tucking into a hearty breakfast before we all took off for a spin on Dad's motorbike—me riding pillion, Mum in the sidecar with Mac, our Scottie mix, curled up at her feet. Maybe we'd be going bluebelling in nearby Mossy Woods, or farther afield to view the gardens at Sisley, or sightseeing at Hampton Court, alongside the Thames.

Tony's voice drew me back to the present. "Want some?" he asked, proffering the frying pan. But the smell was all I needed. I was still trying to digest the Jungle Rumble.

Leaving Watson to be entertained by Trixie, we took off for Bobbi's trailer.

Mary, the beleagured pit bull, was tied up in the back-yard, and gave no warning of our approach. In fact, she seemed pleased to see us, gratefully licking my hand as I filled her empty water bowl from a garden hose.

We knocked first, just in case Bobbi had changed her plans. There was no response, and while I held the flash-light, Tony proceeded to pick the lock, displaying skills that certainly hadn't grown rusty during his professed retirement.

"Do be careful," I said as he worked. "Don't damage the door or break anything."

Tony looked up at me, blinking in the beam of the flashlight. "Don't worry, luv. I've done this more times than you've 'ad 'ot dinners."

"Maybe so; and no doubt been caught a few times, too," I said. "Just be careful."

He ignored the slur on his professionalism, and, com-pleting his task, pushed the door open and palmed me in with a broad grin.

" 'Allo!" he called. "Anyone 'ome?"

"Only me," answered a frail voice.

"Fred?" said Tony. "Where are you, mate?"

"Over here," came the answer from the far end of the room, where Fred sat in his rocking chair.

He told us Bobbi had locked him in while she was away.

"She left me a peanut-butter-and-jelly sandwich, and a thermos of cocoa," he said. "She said she didn't want me wandering off, like I do sometimes," he explained matter-of-factly.

I guessed this wasn't the first time he'd been left alone like this.

He got stiffly out of his rocker. "Nothing to worry

about. Bobbi said she'll be back tomorrow."

"Monstrous," I said. "Nothing to worry about, indeed! The wicked woman. What if there was an emergency, a fire or an earthquake? Supposing he'd become ill?"

"It's bad all right," said Tony. "But keep yer voice down. You'll get us shopped."

He was right; I didn't need to make a commotion and alert the neighbours. But I was determined at the very first opportunity to discover Fred's family and give them the rough side of my tongue for leaving their elderly relative in such irresponsible care.

"Where's the ankle biter?" asked Tony, looking around for the poodle.

"She took Spike with her," said Fred. "She took my gloves, too."

"Gloves?" I asked.

"My gloves that I feed the seagulls with. She took them the other day, and never gave them back, never gave them back." His voice faded as he repeated the phrase.

I promised him that if she didn't return them soon, I would make it my business to get him another pair.

From what I could see by the flashlight, the main living area was in much the same mess as it had been in the last time I visited. Dishes piled up in the sink, a heavy layer of dust over the furniture, and that same unpleasant odour, sour, with a trace of cheap perfume, that had pursued me ever since I'd taken on this case, still hung in the air.

The birds, who had started to fuss in their cages as soon as we walked in, looked like the same assortment also, except that the African grey was gone. In its place was a scarlet macaw.

I pointed it out to Tony. "Is it the one you're looking for?" he asked.

"There's no way of telling. They all look alike to me. Mrs. Handley would know, but we can't bring her over here."

"I wonder how Bobbi plans to unload it," said Tony.

Fred chimed in. "She's going to take all the birds to the swap meet tomorrow. She said she's got to turn them around quick, 'cause she needs the cash for Little Bob's bail."

"I'll get Mrs. Handley to come to the swap meet, then," I said. "I'll make out like I'm going to buy the bird, and she can tell me if it's Scarlett O'Hara. If it's not, I'll simply pretend to change my mind and walk away."

"And if it is?" said Tony.

"We'll accuse Bobbi of stealing it. She'll have to back down. She won't make a fuss if we threaten to call the police."

Making sure Fred was comfortable for the night, we locked him in again. I wasn't at all happy about leaving him, but he was obviously afraid of Bobbi's wrath, and became quite alarmed when we suggested doing otherwise. Tony promised me he would check on the old man later that night, then again first thing in the morning, before he went surfing.

"Now, you be sure not to tell Bobbi we were here," I said to Fred as we closed the door.

He put his finger to his lips. "Mum's the word," he whispered.

As I was shining the flashlight to show our way, I spotted a couple of cobalt-blue feathers lying just beneath the trailer steps.

I pulled on Tony's arm. "Here, look at this."

Together we followed a trail of blue feathers down the porch steps, and through the backyard to the covered aviary that Bobbi had pulled me away from during my first visit.

" 'Alf a mo'," said Tony, reaching to draw aside the heavy tarpaulin cover. "Blimey."

Together we gazed at two beautiful blue macaws, blinking in the sudden light. " 'Ere's yer bloomin' 'Y-acinths."

I spotted a few red feathers on the bottom of the cage also. "I bet this is where she kept the scarlet macaw till she got the Hyacinths. Then after she got rid of the African grey, she transferred the scarlet to the house."

"Regular musical chairs—or perches—she's been playing," agreed Tony, nodding. " 'Ave a look-see in the shed and see if you can find a cage. We may as well take these back where they came from."

Caution overcame me. "But what if they're not the right ones?"

"A course they're the right ones," scoffed Tony. " 'Ow many bleeding blue birds worth thirty thousand grand do you think there are in Surf City, or in all of Southern California, come to that? And with 'er reputation . . ." He was getting impatient with me. "What's the matter with you? Losing your bottle?"

I stood my ground. "No. I haven't lost my nerve, thank you very much. But I'm not going to resort to stealing, even if it probably is stolen property to begin with. I'll report it to Detective Mallory, and let him sort it out."

"Okay, Miss Bossy Boots, 'ave it your way," he said, covering up the cage again.

"I intend to. Come on, let's get out of here."

But before we left, I petted Mary again, and looked

around for some fresh kibble for her. I found it in the storage shed. Found, too, just inside the door where they appeared to have been carelessly thrown, Fred's gloves, a rip down the seam of the right-hand index finger, the exposed lining blotched with what might have been blood. They lay atop a long iron bar, the kind used to change car tires, but which I suspected had been used recently for a more sinister purpose. In the dim illumination afforded by the flashlight I could see that it, too, was daubed with blood.

I RANG MALLORY'S office as soon as I got home, intending, indeed hoping, not to speak to him but to leave a message with the desk sergeant. Unfortunately, Mallory was still there, apparently having given up on his dinner plans.

How to announce myself? "Delilah" sounded too friendly. "Mrs. Doolittle" not friendly enough. I played it safe and compromised. "Delilah Doolittle here."

"Did you change your mind? It's a little late."

He sounded hopeful, and I was once again overcome with guilt.

How to put this? "No. Actually, I was visiting friends this evening"—true enough, Tony and Fred were both friends—"and I happened to learn that someone has very recently acquired a couple of Hyacinth macaws under questionable circumstances."

"Who is this someone?"

"Bobbi Briscoe."

"Any relation to Little Bob Briscoe?"

"His mother, actually. They live together out at the Surf City Trailer Park."

"Thanks. I'll check it out." He paused. "Lucky you heard about it."

There might have been just a hint of sarcasm in his voice, but I let it pass. I was not about to tell him that luck had nothing to do with it.

I didn't mention the tire iron, either. He'd find it when he searched Bobbi's place. After all, I had to leave him something to discover for himself. I wouldn't want to embarrass him by having him think I'd solved his case for him.

· 20 ·

Tickety Boo

THE SWEEPING GENERALIZATION that things seldom turn
out as badly as might have been expected was once
again proven fallacious when, already on edge about
what the day might hold, my nerves were further tested
by Evie's arrival moments before I was to depart for the
swap meet.

She was fairly over the moon, full of schemes to get
Senator Farley Wellstock to come to the point.

"I've got it all worked out," she said, dumping Chamois in his carryall on the kitchen table, almost knocking
over my second-best china teapot in her excitement.
"We'll open up The Frenshams next month," she continued, referring to her and Howard's place in the Bahamas, "and you will both be houseguests. It's so
romantic—the moonlight, palm trees, quiet beaches.
Howard and I spent our honeymoon there. Farley's
bound to pop the question. It will be such a relief to
have you settled at last."

She lifted Chamois out of his bag and placed him in
her lap. Then: "Is that what you're wearing?" she asked,
regarding me critically.

The weather was warm, and I thought my green camp

shirt, tan shorts, and sandals an appropriate outfit for a swap meet. But it wouldn't have done for the shopping spree Evie had planned to the Dior Boutique at South Coast Plaza, lunch at the Ritz, then on to Neiman Marcus at Fashion Island, one of the southland's most exclusive fashion enclaves.

Her own ensemble wouldn't have been out of place at a society wedding. Accessorizing an expertly tailored charcoal-grey knit dress and matching coat, she wore black patent court shoes and a shiny black straw boater which covered most of her short ash-blond hair.

I complimented her on the hat.

"You like it?" she asked, pulling an engraved silver compact from her purse and regarding her image. "Actually, it's hiding a multitude of sins. The roots are due for a touch-up next week."

She nattered on about the senator as she proceeded to freshen her make-up.

"It'll be just tickety boo, having you in the social whirl," she said, expertly applying lipstick in just the right shade of coral.

Oh yes, just peachy keen, I'm sure, I thought.

"You'll be in Washington while Congress is in session, of course," she continued, "and I will come and visit, to help you host all those divine politicos."

Rummaging in her black patent handbag she retrieved a long silver cigarette holder, matching lighter, and a cigarette case containing her favorite Sobranies. "Then there'll be campaigning at home. Of course, Texas is a little stark," she added, lighting up and blowing smoke all over the kitchen. "But the house itself lacks for absolutely nothing. It will be quite marvelous for entertaining."

Watson sneezed at the smoke, and I pointedly opened the kitchen window.

She planted a lipsticky kiss on Chamois's head as another thought struck her. "And . . . he has dogs, too!" She was quite delighted with herself at this piece of information, obviously convinced that the possession of one or more canines would be all that would be required of any man intent on persuading me to fall into his arms.

"Yes. Pointers. I believe he hunts," I said disapprovingly when I could get a word in edgewise. "And he has two children."

"Oh, don't quibble over details," she said crossly. "They'll be away at school or with their mother most of the time."

I tried to get her off the subject of the senator by showing her the latest addition to my household.

"A bird! What are you thinking? Another mouth to feed. Really, Dee. Your compulsion to take in every creature that crosses your path borders on the pathological. I'm quite sure the senator won't approve."

Evie always has been prone to exaggeration in order to make a point. She had made similar comments before—about Saki the Shih Tzu, Hobo the three-legged feral, and Watson's rescue kittens for which we had eventually, and not without a great deal of effort, managed to find good, responsible indoor homes. There had also been the "muttley" crew of cockerpoos, a legacy from a previous case, that had similarly taken weeks of painstaking effort to place.

But fortunately Evie chose not to dwell on my weakness for displaced animals. Today the senator dominated her thoughts, as evidenced by her next remark.

"You'll sell this place, of course," she said, looking

around disparagingly at my humble abode, "so at least you won't be going empty-handed."

She seemed to have thought of everything, right down to my dowry.

"I won't be going anywhere," I said, trying to stem the torrent of her enthusiasm.

"Why ever not?"

I ticked off the reasons on my fingers. "One, I don't see myself as a politician's wife. Or anybody's wife, come to that." I consider husbands rather a nuisance, except when it comes to heavy lifting and fixing the car. "Two, I don't want to get married. And three, I don't care for him."

Evie's light brown eyebrows shot up in surprise. "Don't care for him? But he's a senator."

"Oh, but I've never thought of myself as caring for senators," I said rather wildly, searching desperately for something to shut her up. Evie's enthusiasm was beginning to pall.

"I'm not asking you to *like* the man. Just marry him, and finally have some security in your life." She frowned. "After all I've done to find you a RNM, I think you might be a little more appreciative."

I hated to make her cross, and I didn't want to put her in a pout for the remainder of the day. After all, she had made a considerable, albeit unasked for, effort on my behalf. "We'll see," I said in a more conciliatory tone. "Anyway, he hasn't proposed yet. But shopping's not on today. I have to go to the swap meet at the county fairgrounds."

"Whatever for?"

"To look for a scarlet macaw."

"Why not get one from a pet shop?"

We seemed to be on different planets. "I'm working a case," I said, going on to explain, as briefly as possible, that I was on the trail of a stolen pet.

"But you've no need to work anymore," she said, glancing around for an ashtray. Before I had a chance to look in the cupboard for something suitable, she reached over and tapped the ash into the sink. "Your working days are over. You'll soon have a wealthy husband."

I refused to get into any further argument about my wedding plans. "Be that as it may, I am in the middle of this case, and I must see it through," I said firmly as I turned on the tap and washed the offending ash down the drain.

Never one to take a hint unless it suited her, Evie lit another cigarette, deep in thought. She knew me well enough to know that I wouldn't leave a case unfinished, not even for lottery millions. She brightened. "You know, I've heard there are hidden treasures to be found at swap meets. Family heirlooms, antiques, and the like going for a song. I'll come with you. It'll be a lark."

More of a lark than she knew, I figured. But it was useless to try to dissuade her, once her mind was made up. So with Watson and Chamois on the back seat of her sporty silver Mercedes convertible, their little black noses pointing into the wind, we headed for the fairgrounds.

"Nothing would get me into that death trap of yours," she said, regarding my ancient station wagon in the driveway with distaste. "But we won't have to worry about that for long. You'll soon be trading it in on a Jag. Be sure to get that British racing green. Lovely with your red hair."

I hardly paid her any attention. I was much more concerned about whether Fred might have told Bobbi of Tony's and my visit to her trailer the night before. If Bobbi had been tipped off, the jig was up.

• 21 •

Born to Be Wild

TONY AND TRIXIE were waiting at the swap-meet entrance.

Tony was delighted to see Evie again. "Hallo, Mrs. C. I knew you couldn't keep away from me for long," he greeted, his grey eyes dancing.

Always ready to enjoy a mild flirtation, Evie clasped him warmly. "Of course, dear boy," she said, beaming under his admiration.

We were soon joined by Beryl Handley, who came riding along on her three-wheeler with Saki, the Shih Tzu, in a basket on the front handlebars, his wavy black-and-white coat blowing in the light afternoon breeze.

I had called Beryl the previous evening. She was excited to be part of the scheme, all agog in anticipation of the return of Scarlett.

"It just has to be her," she'd said when I'd cautioned her to be prepared for disappointment. "You're such a smart girl, you wouldn't be doing this unless you were sure."

I hoped I would be able to justify her confidence.

Holding Tony's arm, Evie seemed to be enjoying herself. "What curious ways people have of passing the time," she said, pulling down the brim of her boater to shade her eyes and gazing around at the crowded outdoor marketplace. Weekend bargain hunters jostled at stalls catering to every taste. At a health-food bar people lined up for a free sample of carrot juice. Produce stands laden with fresh-picked crops offered fresher, bigger, and cheaper fruit and veggies than the supermarkets; the smell of fresh strawberries made me promise myself to pick up a couple of baskets before leaving. Knockoff brands of sunglasses and perfumes and bootlegged videotapes were ready sellers. At a used-book stall collectors hunted through tattered paperbacks and outdated encyclopedias for that elusive first edition.

A jewelry stall near the entrance caught Evie's eye. I could tell she was itching for a closer look, and I was more than willing to let her wander off on her own, out of my hair.

What I hadn't bargained for was that she would talk Tony into going along with her.

Tony had readily agreed. "Got to watch yerself in these places. I'd better come along to make sure you don't get rooked," he said as he ushered Evie through the throng. " 'Ang on to yer bees and 'oney," he continued, using Cockney rhyming slang for "money."

And before I had a chance to argue, I found myself standing there with Chamois in my arms and Trixie on a leash, alongside Watson.

Abandoned by my partner-in-crime, and lumbered with the three dogs, I trundled after Beryl, who had hurried on ahead, eagerly on the lookout for a bird vendor.

Making our way through the crowds was slow going. We were a hazardous pair: Beryl, pushing her trike, had difficulty avoiding running it into the shins of the other shoppers, while I had my work cut out trying to keep

Watson and Trixie's leashes from tripping passersby.
More congestion was caused when people stopped first
to pet Saki, and then, having covered only a few feet,
to fuss over Chamois. They usually gave Watson a wide
berth, while Trixie was far too skittish to stand still for
a second.

We eventually spotted a blue-and-white canopy from
which hung a homemade sign announcing EXOTIC BIRDS
& SUPPLY'S. The motorbike-sidecar-trailer rig parked
alongside the booth indicated we had come to the right
place.

Bobbi, decked out in what appeared to be the same
khaki shorts and black tank top she'd worn the first day
I met her, leaned back in a folding chair behind the stall,
drinking a beer, the chubby fingers of her left hand dip-
ping nachos into a repulsive-looking mixture of melted
cheese and salsa. A grubby bandage covered her right
hand. Spike the poodle was curled up on a green velvet
cushion in a basket by her side.

On the table in front of the stall were several cages
containing parakeets, cockatiels, and finches, together
with a glass fishbowl and a sign that read PLEASE HELP
RESCUED BIRDS. A lone dollar bill rested in the bottom
of the bowl. Seed money deposited by Bobbi herself, no
doubt, in hopes of raising bail for Little Bob.

And there, on a perch in the centre of the table, sat
the scarlet macaw.

We had barely reached the stall before Beryl clutched
my arm with her free hand (the other holding the tricycle) and cried out, "That's her! That's my Scarlett
O'Hara. I'd know her anywhere."

Bobbi had watched our approach with that gleam in
the eye common to merchants the world over when they
spot a likely customer. As she came out of the shade of

the canopy, she wrinkled her eyes in the sun, and I don't think she recognized me at first.

The original plan had been for Tony to chat her up and smooth the way while I would feign interest in purchasing the bird, then question Beryl in a quiet aside. But my accomplice was still nowhere to be seen, and Beryl had already tipped our hand.

Bobbi responded angrily to her outburst. "I got this bird from a reputable dealer."

I spoke up. "And who was that, may I ask? Do you have an invoice?"

It must have been my accent, for at this point Bobbi recognized me. "Oh, it's you," she said with a sneer.

Ignoring, perhaps unwisely, her belligerent tone, I said, "What's the name of the dealer?"

She hesitated a moment or two, no doubt considering her options, before saying, "Sweet Tweets." Probably the only dealer's name she knew.

She was lying. I was sure Vance would never deal in stolen birds. And anyway, he had raised Scarlett O'Hara from a fledgling and would have recognized her instantly if she had come into his hands from another source.

"That's not true," cried Beryl. "That's my Scarlett."

The macaw, meanwhile, had brightened up at the sight of her mistress and the Shih Tzu. Blinking beady eyes, she started squawking, "Good boy, Saki. Saki's a good boy," over and over again.

By then a crowd had gathered, whether drawn by the bird's chatter or Beryl's shouted accusations, I couldn't be sure. But it was enough to get Bobbi rattled.

She came around to the front of the stall. "Why don't you mind your own goddam business?" she yelled inches from my face, overwhelming me with her beer breath and her cheap perfume. Then she pushed me into

Beryl, who, in turn, tumbled into the three-wheeler, causing Saki to leap out in fright and run for cover. Next, first grabbing the macaw from its perch, then bending to swoop up the startled Spike, Bobbi backed out of the rear of the stall and fled on foot—poodle under one arm, macaw under the other.

By the time I'd recovered myself, helped Beryl to her feet, righted the trike, and retrieved Saki, Bobbi had a considerable head start.

I looked around in desperation, and my eye fell on the only mode of transit available: the Harley. Hastily bundling Watson, Chamois, and Trixie into the sidecar, I hopped on the motorbike, memory flooding back from my youth of how to start it. I jumped on the starter, put in the clutch, and the engine roared to life. I took off in pursuit of the bird thief, only dimly aware of Beryl pedaling furiously along behind me.

I soon realized why Bobbi had not chosen the motorbike for her getaway. Hampered by the sidecar, it was almost impossible to maneuver the rig through the crowds. People leaped out of the way as I careened up one aisle and down another, with Watson, Chamois, and Trixie barking excitedly, as if to cheer me on.

The orange-crate trailer was the first casualty. As I whipped around a corner by the produce stall, the flimsy chain broke loose as it hit the canopy's metal upright. My promised strawberries were mashed into a messy jam.

A security truck joined in the chase when, after swerving—unsuccessfully—to avoid a stall piled high with soccer balls, I knocked down a sign near the entrance which read MOTORIZED VEHICLES PROHIBITED BEYOND THIS POINT. In the side mirror I glimpsed Tony, skinny legs hopping between the bouncing balls, heading first one, then kneeing another out of the way of the startled onlookers as he desperately tried to catch up with me.

By the time I saw the police car, it was too late to avoid a crash. Through the car's windshield I caught sight of Mallory's face, all confusion and alarm, as the bike slid alongside, the left handlebar scoring a deep impression in the paintwork.

The bike finally came to a halt when it smashed into the entrance barrier, the impact causing the sidecar to snap off. The bike rolled over on me and I felt a searing pain as the hot exhaust pipe pressed against my bare leg.

I watched helplessly as the sidecar trundled away carrying Watson, Saki, and Chamois with it.

· 22 ·
Casey's Court

EVIE, WHO ALL this time had remained at the jewelry stall by the entrance, rushed to my side, joined in short order by Detective Mallory.

I grasped Evie's arm. "The dogs. Quick, save them." The sidecar had come to rest against the fence, and thus far only Trixie had ventured to jump out. Watson sat quietly waiting for a command, and while Chamois wasn't visible, my guess was that he was a little ball of bewilderment huddling in the bottom of the sidecar.

While Evie rushed to collect the dogs, Mallory helped me to my feet. "Bobbi Briscoe," I gasped, pointing to a spot outside in the car park where I could clearly see Tony and Beryl still chasing after the bird thief. "She's getting away!"

Mallory quickly dispatched Offley to apprehend her, then, having satisfied himself that I was all in one piece, turned his attention to sorting out the shambles I had created.

After a brief visit—at Mallory's insistence—to St. Mary's Hospital emergency room, I was firmly invited by the young officer accompanying me to return with him to the police station.

Surf City PD headquarters was located in the old part of town in the city-hall complex. It was across the street from a small park which provided a pleasant getaway for city staff on their lunch breaks. I looked longingly at my favourite picnic spot under a huge oak tree, before the officer hustled me into the police station squad room.

There I found, to use an expression from an old English comic strip, a "Casey's court" in progress. Or, also of British origin, bedlam.

Everyone appeared to be talking at once, each giving a slightly different version of what had transpired, depending on where they had been at the time.

Tony, who had caught up with Bobbi first and held on to her and the macaw long enough for "that geezer Offley" to puff up and make the arrest, was loud in his opinion that if it hadn't been for him, the woman would have got clean away.

The sports-equipment vendor, intent on filing a complaint against Tony for stealing his soccer balls on the pretext of trying them out in the aisle, conferred about legal options with the owner of the produce stall, while a representative from the fairgrounds management demanded to know who would be liable for the damage to county property.

Emotions ran high. Beryl clutched Scarlett to her bosom, Scarlett clung to Beryl, who, with tearful indignation, insisted that the macaw be returned to her immediately. Bobbi, just as vehemently, though less convincingly, claimed legal ownership.

At one point when Sergeant Offley threatened to arrest Beryl, the macaw squawked in his face, causing the burly policeman to back off a step or two, trampling the toes of an elderly woman, who, having apparently wandered into the wrong department by mistake, was asking if this was where she could get her half-price senior-citizen dog license.

Overall, Evie's piercing upmarket tones could be heard talking on her cell phone. "Get Max here straight-away, Howard. I have no intention of allowing Delilah to spend the night in chains. But promise me, darling, not a word to the senator."

Her outfit no longer looked so elegant: torn hose, straw hat askew, a large oil stain on the coat, no doubt from the motorbike. At some point she had removed her black patent court shoes, which now rested in Mallory's "out" basket.

The detective asked her politely to put down the phone and answer his questions. "I think I've met you before, haven't I?" he said, frowning.

"I'm not on file, am I?" she said. "How absolutely thrilling." She took a cigarette from the silver case. "You don't happen to have a light on you, do you?" she asked him.

Apparently words failed him.

She had retrieved Watson, Trixie, and Chamois un-harmed, and now, she quickly reassured me, they, along with Saki, were all safe in her Mercedes in the police parking garage—with the top up, of course. I shuddered to think what damage Trixie might be wreaking on the rag top in her anxiety to reach Tony.

Mallory and Offley tried to sort out the facts from the conflicting accounts, but it was Scarlett O'Hara McCaw herself who finally settled the ownership dispute, re-sponding to several of Beryl's commands, and finally, when Bobbi claimed for the umpteenth time that she had obtained the bird legitimately, screeching, "Frankly, my dear, I don't give a damn!"

Confronted with this indisputable evidence, Bobbi at

last conceded ownership to Beryl, offering to sell the bird back to its rightful owner "at my cost" of five hundred dollars, which, she pointed out magnaminously, was the amount of the reward we had offered.

Pressed to reveal how she had come by the bird, she laid the blame squarely on her son, though she stuck to her story that she didn't know how it came into his hands. She was held without bail until her son could be brought in for questioning.

To refuse bail seemed a bit harsh for the crime of bird theft, and I could only guess at the reasons: by implicating her son, Bobbi was now a material witness in a murder case, not to mention being a prime suspect in the robbery and assault at Sweet Tweets. Mallory had more legwork to do before any further charges could be filed, and Bobbi represented a flight risk. None of which information the detective was at liberty to reveal at that time.

As the young officer escorted her out, Bobbi shrugged off his hand and paused in front of me. "As for you," she said with a sneer. "Don't think you're getting away with wrecking my Harley. I'm filing charges for theft."

Tony saw my dismay. "Don't worry about it, luv," he said kindly. "She's got a lot more to worry about than that ol' bike of her'n. I'll see if I can't get one of me mates to patch it up for her. Any old 'ow, she won't be needing it for quite a while where she's going."

Tony seemed to be blessed with any number of mates capable of a variety of skills, but I was rather afraid that Bobbi's motorbike, not in the greatest condition to begin with, was now quite possibly beyond anybody's talent to repair.

Finally, Sergeant Offley having, with his customary

gloomy stoicism, collected the names and addresses of all present, we were told we could leave. Whereupon it was universally agreed that a cup of tea was absolutely essential, and we all adjourned to my house.

· 23 ·

Home to Roost

IT WAS NICE to be coddled. I sat on the sofa with my feet up while Evie made tea and Beryl plumped up the cushions behind my back and tucked Great-aunt Nell's knitted afghan around my legs—or at least, around the leg that wasn't bandaged.

I had been extremely fortunate that my injuries were no worse. *Cuts and bruises, first-degree burn on left calf,* the emergency-room report had stated.

I looked around anxiously. "Watson . . ."

"Right here, dear," said Beryl, pointing behind the sofa, where my dog was playing tug-of-war with my slipper with her friend Saki.

Indeed, dogs seemed to be everywhere. At the sound of her name, Watson came over and laid her head on the sofa within reach of my hand. Saki and Chamois were under everybody's feet, trying to stay as close as possible to their respective mistresses, while Trixie, true to family form, mooched my best Walker's shortbread from Tony's hand.

Meanwhile, from the top of Dolly's cage, Scarlett O'Hara McCaw held forth with "All's well that end's well," repeatedly, while, not to be outdone, the cockatiel responded with her own fractured version of "Hello, Dolly."

"So it was Scarlett who solved the crime in the end," I said.

Evie poured more tea. "Yes, but can you believe that lout of a police constable—what's his name? P. C. Awfully?—had the cheek to try to take the credit? He was only able to arrest that dreadful Briscoe woman because Tony, the dear boy, held her down for him!

"And the fuss that detective person made about getting you to the hospital! I told him, 'I can take care of my friend, thank you very much.' But he would have none of it. Sent an officer instead. I think he would have gone himself if he could have got away."

She left to answer the telephone, which had been ringing practically nonstop for the last half an hour. Reporters after a story, irate swap-meet merchants seeking damages. If any of my business clients had been trying to get through they'd have been out of luck. So would I. I was going to need all the business I could muster to remedy the fallout from this unfortunate caper.

Tony came over and sat on the edge of the sofa and elaborated on what I had missed.

"What about the Hyacinths?" I asked.

"Dunno," he said. "But Mallory'll get to the bottom of it, I daresay."

"If Bobbi and Little Bob go to jail, what's to be done about their dogs, Spike and Mary?" I asked him.

"No problem. That there bloke from animal control, Mike Denver, was there. They'd been called in 'cause of all Bobbi's birds being left at her stall at the swap meet. I told 'im as 'ow we—you and me, that is—would be 'appy to take care of the dogs. I'll take the pit, and you can 'ave the poodle. Just temp'ry, mind," he added hastily as I started to protest. "Just till the Briscoes can make permanent arrangements."

"What about Bobbi's birds, though? How will they be able to tell which were hers, and which might have been stolen?"

"That's up to animal control. Mike said he'll hold 'em for a decent period of time, put an ad in the paper to give the owners a chance to go to the shelter and claim them, and then they'll go up for auction, like usual."

"And Fred!" I gasped, suddenly remembering the elderly gent. "What about poor old Fred? You don't think Bobbi left him locked up again, do you?"

"Not to worry, luv," Tony answered, patting my good leg. "I went by 'is family's 'ouse this morning and told them they'd better make other arrangements."

There were still many unanswered questions, but my friends seemed to run dry on information, and I was beginning to tire of all the company. Beryl made the motherly suggestion that it was time for me to rest, and with Scarlett perched on her shoulder, and Saki tucked under her arm she left soon afterward.

Tony and Trixie followed a short time later. "TTFN, luv," he said. "Looks like you've got more company coming. I'll leave the door open."

Evie hung up the telephone, having concluded a spirited conversation with someone.

"That was the *Times*," she said. "I told them 'no comment,' and that you were unavailable to talk to them. We have to keep it out of the papers. The senator won't like this at all. It's going to take all my powers of persuasion to talk him 'round. It won't be good for his career if it leaks out that his fiancée has been mixed up in a scandal."

"If by 'fiancée' you're referring to me, he has nothing to worry about," I retorted sharply.

She brought the telephone over to the sofa and placed it within my reach. "Well, I'm off. We have dinner plans this evening. I can't say it's been fun, but . . ." Her unspoken criticism of recent events hung in the air as she gathered up Chamois and his sport bag. "Thank heavens you have Tony to keep you out of any more mischief."

Before I could think of an appropriate response to that barb, there was a light rap on the door. We looked up to see Mallory standing in the open doorway.

• 24 •

Is It a Date?

EVIE LOOKED AT the detective doubtfully, then said, "Will you be all right, Dee? I can hang on a little bit longer if you like, but I did promise Howard I'd be home before dark."

I assured her I would be quite safe with Surf City's finest.

"Well, if you're sure." Then, with a sidelong glance at Mallory, "Don't worry, I'll sort things out with the senator. See you in the Bahamas!" And in a cloud of airborne kisses she was gone.

Mallory watched as she walked to her car, then turned to me and said with a grin, "Coast clear?"

I suspected he had waited until he'd seen the mob depart before knocking on the door.

He petted Watson, who had got up to greet him. He must have changed before coming over. I hoped he wouldn't get dog hair all over his nice dark navy suit. With a white shirt and light blue tie, he looked more like he was dressed for a date than for duty. But no doubt he was here for another of his wretched statements, and maybe to deliver a bill for the damaged police cruiser as well. Not to mention a lecture on the follies and perils of interfering with police business.

But he was surprisingly silent on that topic. "How are you feeling? If this is a bad time, I can come back later," he said.

"No, really. I'll be right as ninepence in no time. I just need to stay off my feet for a while," I said. Then, remembering my manners: "Do sit down." I indicated the armchair facing the sofa, where I could see him without having to change my position. "Did you find the Hyacinth macaws?"

"Yes. Thanks for the tip. Along with other evidence linking the Briscoe woman to the Sweet Tweets break-in."

I knew you would was my unspoken rejoinder, remembering the bloodstained gloves and tire iron.

"We've also made arrangements with U.S. Customs to bring the son in for questioning. Following the identification of Mrs. Handley's stolen bird, he's now a murder suspect."

"Murder. You mean José Martinez?"

He reached into the inside pocket of his jacket for his notebook. "From what we've been able to piece together so far, with the Briscoe woman's help—she's cooperating to save her own skin—she and Fidel Gomez have been running a bird-smuggling operation, using Martinez and Briscoe Junior as couriers. From the evidence, it looks like Little Bob killed Martinez in a fight over a side deal they had going. They saw the escalating market for exotic birds, got greedy, and they weren't content with smuggling anymore. That's when they started to steal pets and locally raised birds."

"Much more in demand than wild-caught," I put in.

"Right," he said. "We figure they probably got into a fight over your scarlet macaw, which they'd stolen, Martinez ended up dead, and young Briscoe dumped him in the ocean off Sunset Beach."

"What about Gomez?" I asked. "Were you able to track him down?"

"Our sources tell us he's back in Mexico. Apparently he gave up the chase in San Diego."

"Good old Evie," I murmured.

"Customs tells us they've been trying to build a case against him for years. Bobbi Briscoe's confession might be all they need."

He leaned down and picked up a red feather from the floor. "Is this from the stolen macaw?" I nodded as he continued, "Maybe we'll be able to get more evidence from a DNA test, comparing the feather we found on the victim, this one, and those in Martinez's truck."

It was all coming together now. "Bobbi must have had Scarlett O'Hara all along, hidden in the aviary in her backyard. I spotted a few red feathers when I discovered the Hya—" I closed my mouth abruptly. I had nearly let slip a mention of my breaking-and-entering escapade the previous evening.

Mallory looked stern. "I know you were there," he said.

"How do you know that?" I said defensively.

He shrugged. "I'm a detective. It's my business to know things."

"Actually, I . . ." I had been about to deny it, but considered the futility of it all, concluding that if I was to be arrested for breaking and entering, I would just have to suffer the consequences, doing my best to keep Tony out of it. The authorities would be much harder on him than on me, a first-time offender.

Mallory had raised bushy eyebrows inquiringly, waiting for me to finish my sentence.

". . . I can practically taste the bread and water," I finished lamely, hoping he could take a joke.

Apparently he could. Or possibly how I came to discover the Hyacinths wasn't a line of inquiry he was prepared to pursue just then. After jotting something in his notebook, he went on to explain that acting on my tip, he had got a search warrant and earlier that morning had gone to Bobbi's trailer, where he discovered the Hyacinths. "An old guy was hanging around there—"

"Must have been Fred," I put in.

He ignored my interruption. "He told us that Bobbi was at the swap meet. I was on my way there to arrest her for the assault and robbery at Sweet Tweets when I ran into you." He smiled. "Or, rather, you ran into me."

I looked away in embarrassment.

"Anyhow, after questioning, she confessed to the break-in, and with a promise of easier sentencing, she told us about her son's involvement with José Martinez. And, as I said, we pieced together the rest."

He must have read my mind, for in answer to my unspoken question, he said, "The Hyacinths have already been returned to Sweet Tweets."

"But who's there to take care of them?" I asked with concern.

"DeVayne's sister."

"Vera?"

"Yes. She showed up at the hospital this afternoon. She's been out of town visiting relatives. Only got back today."

"Then she's not involved in any other way?"

"What makes you ask?"

I told him how I had observed her embarrassment each time José's name had been mentioned, and how I had suspected that she might have been involved with him in some way, either romantically, or though it stretched credulity to the limit, in his criminal activities.

Mallory nodded. "That was another reason DeVayne fired him. José'd been making unwelcome advances to her, making a nuisance of himself."

"How's she coping with the news of Vance's brush with death?"

"Shocked, of course. But she seems quite capable of taking care of things at the bird farm."

I would have to give her a ring, and see if there was anything I could do to help. It would be difficult running that big place without Vance.

"And how's Vance doing?"

"He'll be okay. Still critical, but he's conscious, and was able to ID Bobbi Briscoe as his attacker."

"So he's no longer a suspect in the José Martinez murder?"

Mallory shook his head.

"Well, far be it from me to say—" I stopped as he hid a smile. I had been about to say "I told you so," but thought better of it.

Instead, I turned to something else that had been bothering me. "Did Vance tell you why he rang me that night instead of dialing 911?"

Mallory flipped back a couple of pages of his notebook. "He was about to call you to let you know the Briscoe woman had possession of your scarlet macaw and was trying to sell it to him. He recognized it as one of his own hand-raised birds. He had already dialed your number when he was attacked. The last thing he remembers before he passed out was hitting the redial button."

He pocketed his notebook, indicating the interview was over. He made no move to leave, however, but looked at me earnestly. "So you're off to the Bahamas?"

Oh Lord! I had hoped he'd missed that bit of intelligence. "I don't think so. It's Evie's idea, but I really don't have the time right now," I said. I thought he looked relieved.

I must admit, I had been a little tempted by Evie's offer of a free holiday, but not at the price of the senator's company. When the time came, Evie would find I could be just as stubborn as she was. Airline tickets would be politely returned. The senator's advances, should they materialize—which I very much doubted after word of my swap-meet caper got out—would be tactfully rebuffed.

"It sounds like just what you need. A little R 'n' R in the sun," Mallory was saying.

His solicitude seemed genuine, and I realized I had grown rather fond of him lately. He could be arrogant and kind by turns, but all in all, his was a comforting presence. But only in the way I found Bristol Cream sherry and Marmite sandwiches comforting, I told myself hastily. And I knew where I stood with him.

Or thought I did. The ground seemed to be shifting somewhat as he said, "Are you hungry, Delilah? How about dinner?"

"Dinner?" I said as if I'd never heard of the word.

I was about to protest that I wasn't up for it, but he continued, "I know you won't want to go out, but we could order something in. How about that English pub downtown, the Pig 'n' Whistle?"

How thoughtful. He really was rather a dear.

"Yes, Jack," I said, impulsively using his first name, and realizing with a tiny flutter of anticipation that a new stage in our relationship was about to begin. "I'd like that. I'd like that a lot."